This Is a Recording

This Is a
Recording

Barbara Corcoran

Illustrated by Richard Cuffari

Atheneum 1971 New York

1613504

For Helen,
Ralph and Vi

This Is a Recording

ONE

MY FAMILY GAVE ME THIS TAPE RECORDER as a propitiation for their sins, especially the sin of going off to Europe without me and dumping me on my grandmother in the wilds of Montana, a grandmother I haven't seen since I was two, which hardly counts as seeing at all.

The world will little note nor long remember what I say here, but I will one day transcribe this tape into the written word, and when I am old, I will read it with bitterness and rue.

I am recording at the end of the day, which is my custom whenever possible.

This afternoon at three o'clock Eastern Standard Time my parents dumped me in this room at the St. Regis Hotel in New York City. We flew here from Boston on the shuttle but there was no gun play or hijacking, which was rather a disappointment.

"This is the hotel where your grandmother used to live," my mother said very brightly. She has been very bright ever since they told me they were going to Europe without me. She keeps saying things like: "You'll love Montana, darling—you've always had such a thing about cowboys and all that."

With her usual lack of perception she fails to understand that it's one thing to come home from school and put on your gunbelt in the privacy of your own room and practice hip-drawing in the mirror, which I do; and it's quite another thing to be abandoned by your parents in the real West, with a grandmother who used to be an actress until she married this bigshot rancher, and who probably does not remember she even has a grandchild except as an abstraction to whom she sends money for Christmas, like a donation to Christmas seals.

"This is a real old-timer," my father said, meaning the hotel. "Look at that Waterford crystal chandelier."

Actually, as I have discovered while sitting around the room reading the menus, the bar card and the laundry list, this hotel was built in 1904 by John Jacob Astor and the floor in the lobby is some kind of marble that's better than Carrara, that Italian marble that's supposed to be so great. Mr. Astor apparently spat on Carrara and said, "That is not good enough for me." I rode down in the elevator on purpose to see the floor in the lobby. Several people including a bellhop asked me if I had lost something because I was leaning over staring at the floor. There is a big rug but what you can see of the bare floor looks terrible. I think he'd have done better with Carrara. There is also a famous Maxfield Parrish painting in the King Cole Bar but they won't let women in there until evening (why?) and they won't let fourteen-year-old girls in there at any time. From where I stood, the painting looked quite sentimental.

"Now remember, dear," my mother said before they left, obviously dying to get rid of me and be gone, "go down to the dining room and eat a good dinner—a steak or something. All you have to do is sign for it. Daddy has arranged with the manager to put your bill on his American Express card."

My father has a pathological preoccupation with credit cards. The last time I counted, he had seventeen, and he had to get a custom-made leather thing from Mark Cross to hold them all. It makes him walk a little lop-sided, the weight of all those credit cards.

"And do not, absolutely do not, go out of the hotel until you leave for the airport in the morning," my father said.

Not that he needed to worry about that. Everybody knows what happens to you if you walk on the streets of New York alone. Boston is bad enough. We live in Louisburg Square, and I won't even go near the Common. If I could wear my gunbelt, it wouldn't be so bad. There's always that split second when the assailant wouldn't know for sure whether the guns were real or not, and you could use that second to run. My guns do look quite real. They have simulated ivory handles, like General Patton's, only his weren't simulated. But my mother won't let me wear the gunbelt out of the house; it makes her very nervous that I even still have it. I take the view that it's no more retarded than girls who hang onto those stupid stuffed animals, and it might turn out to be a lot more useful.

My mother hugged me and got surprisingly weepy, considering that she's not usually very demonstrative about me. But then my father said, "Come on, we don't want to miss the plane," and he sounded so sharp, she straightened up real quick. He really needed a trip somewhere; he was getting very crabby.

"Give your grandmother a big hug for me," she said, and smiled at herself in the mirror. My mother is quite pretty and if I looked like that, I'd smile, too. Unfortunately, I don't. "Remember to stand up straight, dear," she said, poking my shoulders. I happen to be very round-shouldered, but if any parent ever hears these words, let me implore you not to nag at your children to stand up straight. It does not work. I read somewhere that not all human beings are built to stand up straight, and I believe it.

"Give Katherine a big kiss for me," my father said. They always make a big fuss over her, in absentia, but I don't know how many years it's been since they actually went to see her. We have pictures of her all around the house—Katherine in *Blithe Spirit,* Katherine in *Candida,* Katherine in *Twelfth Night,* etcetera, etcetera. Always the supporting actress, never the star, although Mother says she was "slated for stardom" (that's one of her favorite phrases) until she met Ben Carter and became a rancher's wife. It was a "great loss to the theatre," my mother always says. My father likes to act as if he's spellbound by her, like saying "give Katherine a big kiss for me" and grinning like an idiot—but after all, the woman is sixty-five years old.

"Go to bed early, Marianne," my mother was saying. "And leave plenty of time to get to the airport." She was acting jumpy. She's never liked to travel, and I was surprised that she was going. "The bell captain will get you a cab," my father said.

One of the really neat things about the St. Regis is this antique-looking little house outside where the man who flags down the cabs can stand. It makes you think of horse-drawn cabs with big old horses stamping their feet and blowing out steam on a cold night. I would like to have lived in 1904. To tell you the truth, I am an anachronism.

Well, so they went, and I was left all alone in a city of nine million, give or take a few. I put on my gunbelt right away and turned on TV. I probably should tell here what the news was about because it might one day be of interest to any future historians or anthropologists who happen to come across this account, but the reception wasn't very good and my mind was wandering. I called up a florist and ordered a dozen red roses sent to myself.

It really hit me that I was going to fly about two thousand miles to the real west, to a real grandmother, and I was scared out of my mind. It's one thing to practice hip shots and read *Great Adventures in the Old West* in your nice quiet bedroom in Louisburg Square; it's something else to go there. When I'm really scared, I go to sleep, so I pulled down the bedspread and went to sleep.

When I woke up, I had a sore hip because I had forgotten to take off my gunbelt, and I was terribly hungry. It's not that I'm a hick or anything; I've eaten at the Parker House and the Ritz-Carlton and the Old Union Oyster House and in St. Augustine, Florida, but this was New York. For all I knew, the menu might be entirely in Italian, or French, or maybe even Hungarian. I got

7

out the Room Service list and read it over four times. Finally I got up my nerve to dial Room Service. I was really very hungry, so I ordered two glasses of milk and three cold chicken sandwiches.

I got terribly nervous waiting for the man to come. I cleared everything off the dressing table so he could put the tray down. I could sign the check, but I'd have to tip him. I didn't know how much. Thirty cents seemed like a good round number, so I dug out a quarter and a nickel. I paced the floor, waiting for him.

Then this buzzer sounded. I was expecting a knock, and I was scared out of my mind by the buzzer. I thought it might be a fire drill. But it buzzed again, so I opened the door. There was a very tall waiter, about eight feet tall, and he didn't have a tray at all; he had a pushcart.

"Good evening, Madame," he said. "Room service?"

I lost my cool altogether. I gulped and nodded, and he pushed his big silver pushcart into the room. It had three huge silver-colored dishes, covered, and three glasses of ice water, two glasses of milk, salt and pepper shakers, a dish with three thin slices of pickle (I hate pickles), three napkins humped up to look like Napoleon's hat, a silver bucket of ice and all these knives and forks and spoons. He looked around the room as if he expected more people.

"Would you like it here, miss?"

I noticed he was calling me "miss" now instead of "madame." It's one of those little things that are always happening to me, that can really crush my spirit.

"Yes," I said.

"Your father will sign?" he said, giving me this big false smile. "Your mother?" Again he looked around, although it was obvious to even the most nearsighted person that I was the only human being in the room.

"I will sign." My voice squeaked the way it does in crises. It's a real handicap.

He looked doubtful. "Perhaps your father will be right back?"

"My father," I said, "is on his way to Paris, France. I will sign."

He still hesitated, and I lowered my head the way my mother says makes me look like a young bull about to charge, and without really thinking about it, I put my hand on my left gun. He noticed the gunbelt for the first time, and he paled visibly. I had a great feeling of power. "The pencil, please," I said. He handed it to me, and I signed my name, using my middle initial.

He looked at it carefully, and he still stood there. I remembered the tip. I handed him the quarter and the nickel. He looked down at them as if he had never seen a quarter and a nickel before. Then he glanced at my gunbelt again. "Thank you, Madame," he said, and he left rather quickly.

They were very good chicken sandwiches, and the ice was marvelous. They have an icewater tap but it isn't like real ice that you can crunch. I really had no use for all that silverware, though, and those terrible pickles. I ate the three sandwiches and drank the milk, and that's when I went downstairs to look at the marble floor. Food gives you fortitude.

After I looked at the floor, I went in the drugstore and bought four candy bars and a bottle of shampoo.

On my way up in the elevator there was a bellhop with a box of flowers. I tried to crane my neck to see if they were mine, but he had his arm over the card. I could have asked, but I didn't want him to think that I was naive enough to suppose that no one in New York but me got flowers; so I just marched off the elevator and down the hall to my room, and he marched right along behind me. When I stopped at my door, he stopped.

I turned around with really phoney surprise, and said, "Oh, flowers for me?"

He looked at the card. "Miss Marianne Temple?"

"Yes," I said. "How delightful. Please come in." I was really sickening.

He put them on the dressing table and looked at the card. He seemed a little puzzled. "They were sent collect."

"Yes," I said. "I ordered them for my Aunt Marianne. She's a famous anthropologist. She's on her way here from the Trobriand Islands. How much is it?"

"Twelve dollars and thirty cents." He still looked bewildered, but as long as I was going to pay, it was no worry of his.

I hadn't realized flowers were so expensive. I paid him and remembered to give him a dime for a tip. He had that same funny look the other man had when I tipped him, but then he laughed and said, "Thank you, Miss Temple."

"Quite all right." I swept to the door with my best sweep to open it for him, but I tripped over one of my suitcases and crashed into the wall. He went down the hall chuckling. Some people have a weird sense of humor.

The flowers were already in a vase—no wonder they cost twelve dollars. And there is funny white stuff in the bottom of the vase and a card that says: *Do not remove, Add water daily for long-lasting luxuriant flowers.*

I have taken a shower and washed my hair with my new shampoo, and I am in bed, watching TV.

TWO

I AM IN THE WEST, but first my awful trip. In the morning my travelling alarm clock, another sacrificial offering from my parents, woke me up. I couldn't remember where I was for a minute and I was really scared. There was a terrible racket outside, which turned out to be a gigantic wrecking machine just down the street; it was disemboweling a large building. Auto horns were blowing, a jackhammer was chattering away, and it sounded as if the world had gone insane. My roses were dead. They never even made it out of the bud stage.

I went in the bathroom and washed my face with ice water and I looked in the mirror. At first I thought there was something wrong with the bathroom light. My hair had turned black! I rushed into the bedroom and looked in that mirror. It was black all right. My normal hair is dirty blonde. A hideous thought struck me, and I grabbed the bottle of shampoo. Sure enough, it said, "Ebony Tint." I had dyed my hair! It looked as if I had dumped shoe polish on my head.

It was almost more than I could bear. To punish myself for my stupidity, I looked in the mirror and smiled. That's what I do when I really hate myself. The reason is, my teeth are solid braces. When I smile, all you can see is an expanse of metal. It's enough to blind you. The orthodontist did this to me eight months ago, and I have not smiled more than five times since.

But in spite of this tragedy of the hair, I had to catch that stupid plane for stupid Montana. I had unpacked everything the night before and hung clothes up in the closet and put things in the bureau drawers so I had to repack. Then I had to have breakfast. I got dressed, wearing my new tweed suit and my cowboy boots, and I got out a long white woolen scarf and wrapped it all around my head so no one could see my black hair. It made me look like an Arab.

I ordered Eggs Benedict for breakfast. I had never had them before. They were so good, I thought I'd faint. I ordered a second round, and by the time I got back to my room, I was feeling a little sick. When I'm upset, I make lists, so I made a list: *Finish packing. Call bellhop. Check out. Get cab. Go to Newark airport. Check in baggage. Find gate for Flight 706 to Chicago. (At O'Hare go to Frontier.) Go to the Ladies Room. Take a Dramamine. Board plane.*

Everything was packed, finally, though I had trouble getting my gunbelt in the suitcase; it kept bulging in the wrong places. I got my wallet out and my plane ticket, so I'd have them handy when I needed them. I called for a bellhop.

You always hear about tough talkative New York cab drivers, but mine was a Puerto Rican with eyes like a basset hound and he never said a word all the way to Newark, not even when we were driving through the tunnel under the Hudson River, which I personally thought was pretty wild. How did they build that thing?

I couldn't find a porter at the airport, so I had to carry my own bags and tape recorder to the airline counter. I put my ticket between my teeth. The man laughed when he looked up and saw me. These New York–New Jersey people are real laughing maniacs. I suppose the mad pace unhinges them.

The plane was enormous. I was in First Class, up near the pilot. If we'd been hijacked, I'd have been an eye-witness. I had never flown except on the Boston–New York shuttle. The stewardess smiled and smiled, and insisted on hanging my coat up front somewhere when actually I wanted it with me. I had a lot of things in the pockets that I might need, like aspirin and a package of Sour Strawberry gum and a couple of crossword puzzles that I'd saved from the Boston *Herald*. But when a stewardess makes up her mind to be helpful, you can't stop her.

Also I wanted some paper, so I could make notes about Taking Off in a Jet for the First Time. It's an awesome experience. I kept wondering what Sir Isaac Newton would have said.

Just when we were all revved up and throbbing the length and breadth of the plane, and I was thinking deep thoughts, this other stewardess tapped me on the shoulder and said, "Straighten your seat back for takeoff, dear. It's an FAA rule."

"It won't straighten," I said. I had already tried it.

"Just press the button and give a little spring forward."

The plane was going fast down the runway, and I wanted to experience every second. But you can't fight the FAA. I pushed the button again and sprang forward. Nothing. I tried it again and bumped my nose on the seat in front of me. The seat hadn't budged. The middle-aged man across the aisle leaned across and jerked at the seat. Nothing. The stewardess tried. We were almost airborne and I was going to miss it, fooling with the stupid seat.

"You'll have to move," the stewardess said. "The FAA rule . . ."

I was mad. I got up and kicked the darned thing just as hard as I could with the heel of my boot. The seat sprung into position.

"My God," the man across the aisle said, "that's what my mechanics used to do to my plane in World War Two!"

By the time I could look out the window again, we were in the air. I had missed the whole drama. The man across the aisle wanted to talk some more, probably about World War Two, or about his grandchildren or something, but I gave him my full solid silver smile and that shut him up. I looked down at the ground; the automobiles looked like ants, and the streets were like a design somebody had made with a ruler.

Then we went higher and all you could see was a thick layer of yellow smog. I scrounged around in my purse looking for a piece of paper. I have one of these plastic shields that fit on your breast pocket and I wear that all the time, with about four pencils and three ballpoint pens that clip onto it, and a geometry compass, and a flashlight that looks like a pen. My mother tries to get me to stop wearing it but after all, you never know what you're going to need.

I found a little white paperbag thing in the seat pocket in front of me and I started making notes on that. Then I happened to turn it over and found out what it was for. I threw it under my seat and tried to forget about it.

"Do you want some orange juice?" the stewardess said.

I didn't have the strength for a firm "no" so she misunderstood me and brought me a glass of orange juice. I know of no way to get rid of anything liquid that you don't want, when you're on a plane. If they brought you hemlock you'd have to drink it.

I leaned my forehead against the cold glass of the window. All of a sudden I got this image of my mother standing by the front window in our living room with her forehead against the glass, looking out to the street. It was very cold, there was snow on the hill, and I became my mother, only I couldn't see what it was she was watching so hard, with her shoulders all stiff. Sometimes I think I have ESP. I may turn into a great mystic, with a big crystal ball. I lean my forehead on the crystal ball and it feels cold and there's something I don't want to see, but that's a ridiculous feeling because a mystic's job is to see. They see everything and remain very cool and objective. . . .

"No, thank you, no more orange juice."

You could really enjoy plane travel if they'd only leave you alone. First there's all that jabber that nobody pays any attention to, about oxygen masks; then the pilot comes on like Captain Marvel, telling you about the landmarks you can't see. Then these girls with their smiles and their food. I had already had all those Eggs Benedict and the orange juice, but by actual count I also consumed the following: half a cantaloupe, four muffins with marmalade, two eggs scrambled, two sausages, a bunch of fried potatoes, a cup of coffee and four mint lifesavers. You start eating right out of Newark and before you get a chance to look up from your tray, you're in Chicago.

We were up so high, all you could see was clouds, when you did get a chance to look out the window. I went to sleep for a few minutes and I had this crazy dream that I have sometimes. In the last four years my father has travelled a lot, all over the world, for the leather company he's a partner in. He loves to travel, and he used to try to get my mother to go but she said she couldn't leave me. Actually she didn't want to go; she likes to sleep in her own bed at night. But anyway my father brings us fabulous presents, and once he brought me a big rubber starfish from Macao. It was inflatable. Anyway in my dream, the starfish lies flat on our living room floor and my mother and my father and I stand on its tentacles, holding hands in a circle the way we used to do when I was little, chanting "We three! Nobody is as safe as we!" It sounds ridiculous, but when I was a small child we used to do this and then hug each other and giggle like maniacs. In the dream, though, some sinister unseen force begins to inflate the starfish, and the bigger it gets, the further away from each other we get until we can't hang onto each other's hands any more. And then we're all dumped off and fall into the ocean, and I'm too far away from them to be saved. I woke up from that dream in a cold sweat.

But we were beginning the descent into Chicago so I had other things to think about. I fastened my seat belt so tight I could hardly breathe. We roared at the ground a million miles an hour, and I shut my eyes and waited for the end. The stewardess was yakking away on the intercom, and then I opened my eyes and we were on the ground. I couldn't get my seat belt unfastened, and I was in a panic; I thought I'd be carried to Los Angeles or wherever the plane was going. But the man across the aisle came to my rescue.

I grabbed my coat as the stewardess came up with it, and ran like a deer. O'Hare Airport is about as big as all the New England states put together, and the plane I had to get was, of course, at the farthest away possible place. For miles and miles and miles I ran on cement, with my flight bag and my tape recorder banging me in the knees. I was sure I'd miss the plane.

As it turned out, I had to wait thirty-five minutes before we could board, and twenty minutes more sitting on the runway waiting for a chance to take off. If you want my opinion, the world is overcrowded.

Pretty soon we were airborne, and I discovered that the day was going to be feast and famine. From Chicago to Missoula all I got was a Seven-Up and some hard candy that nearly broke my braces.

At Billings, Montana, I switched to a small two-engine prop plane that looked like something the Wright Brothers threw together to practice on. We flew and flew and flew, and pretty soon a stewardess sat down beside me and said with false enthusiasm, "Is this your first trip to Montana, honey?" She had black hair, and I wondered if it was dyed.

I was feeling like a blob of wet cement, with all that landing and taking off, and I was afraid I might be airsick. "Yes," I said between clenched braces. I looked out the window to cut off conversation but that was a mistake. We were skimming right across the tops of huge jagged mountains, snow-covered even this early. I had never imagined anything so big and empty and scary. If hell was cold, it would look like that. If you crashed in those mountains, it would be like falling on gigantic sawteeth.

Miss Cheerful said, "Then this is your first sight of the Rockies."

"I have never been west of the Hudson River." I was trying to figure how far it was to the ladies' room in case I got any sicker. I'd have to crawl over this airborne welcome wagon on my right and I'd probably trip. I fished in my purse for the Dramamine and couldn't find it. It was probably too late for that anyway.

"Are you parents going to meet you?" She glanced at the white scarf I still had around my head.

I touched the scarf to make sure the ends were tucked in. "My parents are in," I thought for a second, "Morocco. My father is right-hand man to the Sultan."

She looked at me oddly. "How interesting."

"He's the top man in charge of olives."

She decided it was a joke and she laughed politely. She looked at my watch. "You're still on eastern time, sweetie. Mountain time is three hours earlier."

"Actually," I said, "I usually go by Greenwich time." What kind of a world is it when a person can't choose his own time? I'd been on eastern time since birth; why should I be forced to change? But I have no character: I reset my watch.

"Are your relatives going to meet you? Are you visiting?"

I hoped that one large chunk of information would

glut this woman's insatiable curiosity. "I am going to stay with my grandmother, whom I have not laid eyes on since the age of two. She is a former actress, confidante of stars. It is rumored that she slept with John Barrymore. She married a rich rancher and moved to Montana. He is now deceased, and she lives alone in a small town in northwestern Montana." I threw in the bit about John Barrymore but the rest was true.

But of course she didn't believe me; people never believe the truth. She just raised her black eyebrows and said, "Montana is a long way from Morocco." Then we hit an airpocket, and when it was safe to look up again, she was gone.

Pretty soon the intercom began to make funny noises, something like a bell ringing and then squawks and a kind of death rattle. It was a little frightening to be ten thousand feet up in a machine that couldn't even make its intercom work. Then the pilot's voice boomed out. "This is your captain, ladies and gentlemen. We are coming into Missoula, Montana, three minutes ahead of schedule. The skies are sunny, visibility is good, temperature sixty-one degrees. We want to thank you for flying with us at this time, and we hope you enjoyed your trip. When you fly again, please think of us." End of commercial. More squawks, more rattles, and that crazy bell. The bell reminded me of something—what was it? A doorbell ringing in a dark house, two short rings and a long, and then a door opening and closing, and the murmur of voices. I was probably being psychic again; I pushed it out of my mind.

The plane circled and flew at the earth so fast I thought we would all be killed in our seats. Then it touched down, thumped a few times, and taxied to the terminal. I was the first one off the plane, and the black-haired stewardess had to run after me with my coat. I've never in my life made a good exit.

THREE

SO THIS WAS OUT WEST. Actually it was disappointing. Except for being very small, the airport looked like any other airport. And the people were just people. I was the only one in the terminal wearing cowboy boots.

There were about two dozen people, and none of them looked like anybody's grandmother. I went to the door and looked outside. There was a parking lot, like any old parking lot, and some fields. I came back in and got my luggage and waited.

I happened to be looking at the floor—I stare at the floor quite a lot—and I saw this pair of really beat up old boots standing in front of me. I almost didn't bother to look up because it was obviously not going to be my grandmother, but then I got curious about whether it might be a cowboy, so I did look up. The boots belonged to a boy about seventeen or eighteen years old who was looking at me. He seemed to be a cowboy all right— maybe a Mexican cowboy, because his face was quite dark. He had on faded jeans and one of those shirts with little pearl buttons on the pockets. His eyes were black.

"Are you Marianne?" he said.

Well, that really shook me. You don't expect some strange cowboy to call you by name right in the middle of the airport. I didn't know what to say so I pretended I hadn't heard him. He leaned over and looked at the tag on my big suitcase. "Okay," he said. "Come on."

"Come on where?" Life can come up with some really unexpected situations, and I'm not a fast thinker.

He was picking up my luggage. "To your grandmother's," he said, as if I'd asked a dumb question. He strode off toward the parking lot, and you could tell he'd worn those boots a lot because he didn't lose his balance on his heels the way I do on mine.

I didn't know whether to go with him or call the police. For all I knew, he might be in the white slave trade. But I didn't want to lose my bags so I went after him. He was piling them in the back of an old Chevrolet with a mashed fender. Now I knew something was wrong. A woman who has been a supporting actress to Lynn Fontanne wouldn't be driving a car like that.

"Just a minute here," I said. "Where are your credentials?"

He turned to look at me, and right at that moment my white scarf came loose and part of it fell down over my face. I couldn't see a thing. I thought I heard him laugh but I couldn't be sure, and when I got the scarf off, he was standing there beside the door, perfectly serious.

"Why didn't my grandmother come herself?" I said.

"She doesn't know how to drive." He reached in and pulled the car's registration slip off the sun visor and showed it to me. It was my grandmother's name and address, all right. It occurred to me that he might have murdered her and stolen the car, but since he had already gotten in on the driver's side and started the engine, I decided I'd better get in, too. I didn't want to spend the night in the parking lot.

He drove north, away from the city of Missoula, but that was all right because she didn't live in Missoula anyway. He drove fast, hunched over the wheel, with his cowboy hat tipped forward over his eyes. He didn't say a word.

Watching him out of the corner of my eye, it suddenly dawned on me: he wasn't Mexican at all. I said, "Are you a redskin?"

His right eyebrow shot up. That's a trick I've spent many hours trying to master, tilting up one eyebrow like that. It gives you a look of skepticism and superiority and absolute mastery of the situation. But I've never been able to do it.

Without turning his head to look at me, he said, "Me redskin, you paleface."

I was irritated. It wasn't all that funny. "How was I to know? I never saw an Indian before."

"I am ahead of you there. I have seen many paleface."

Another silence. "What's your name?" I said.

"Oliver Everybodylooksat."

"Oh, ha ha ha," I said in my most ironic tone. "You are very, very funny."

He shrugged. Neither of us said anything for a long time. I felt pretty bitter that my grandmother had not come to meet me herself and that she had sent this crazy wise guy.

I decided to maintain a dignified silence the rest of the way.

24

He turned off on a dirt road and he was driving so fast you could hear the gravel spin under the wheels. I hated to think I had come all this way, miles up in the sky, only to be killed by a mad Indian in an old Chevrolet. I concentrated on looking at the scenery. Actually it was quite pretty. Farms and ranches (How do you tell the difference?), fields with groups of cows in them and then lots of woods. You could see the mountains at a distance. I hadn't dreamed you could go so far without seeing a town. The country was so big, it made you feel minute. After quite a while the redskin slowed down as we came into a small town. There was a river running right through the middle of town, and woods just beyond the streets. The sidewalks were wooden walks built up high. I wanted to ask why but I wasn't going to ask *him*.

Whenever I had thought about my grandmother, I'd pictured her living on that big ranch of my grandfather's, although I did really know that in the winter they had lived in town and after he died, she sold the ranch. But I still expected the ranch, and I couldn't believe it when he turned into the driveway of a big old house on a tree-lined street just off the main street. It was kind of a Victorian-looking house, with bay windows and gables. It looked more like civilization than I expected. It was very disappointing. I thought it would be like the house in *Bonanza*.

He took out my bags and waited for me. "Well, aren't you coming?"

"Is this where my grandmother lives?" It could still be a trap. It was common knowledge that a decent woman has always had to look out for sharpers in the Far West.

"Of course," he said. He went up the steps to the big

front door, knocked loudly once, and opened the door.

I followed him, wishing I'd worn my gunbelt. He put my bags down inside the door and jerked his head toward the living room. "She'll be down in a minute." He went out and shut the door.

The hall was dim and cool. I stood close to the door, in case I needed to make a hasty exit. After a couple of minutes a woman appeared at the top of the stairs. It was hard to see her clearly in that light. She was tall and slender, and she was wearing a long dark blue velvet robe. She stood still, looking down at me. A shaft of sunlight came through a round window behind her and lit up her head. She was beautiful. "Marianne?" she said and her voice was one of those low, musical, theater voices, like the record we have of Katharine Cornell in *The Barretts of Wimpole Street.*

"My dear Marianne, how nice." She came down the stairs like Lady Macbeth. It was my grandmother, all right—supporting player to Lynn Fontanne—making her entrance.

When I got a better look, I saw that she was old, after all, and she carried a cane with a carved handle. She had a very slight limp.

"Hello," I said, "Grandmother." I *wish* my voice wouldn't always squeak at historic moments.

She put down the cane and took my face between her hands and kissed me light as a feather on the forehead. She smelled marvelous. It was terrible being scrutinized by someone that beautiful. I knew just how sick she must feel to see what, in the name of a granddaughter, God had wrought. But she only said, "Somehow I thought you were blonde, like your mother."

"I was," I said, "yesterday."

"Come in and sit down. You must be very tired." She swept me into the living room, which was extremely tidy and decorated like a stage set for a Victorian play. I felt too dirty to sit down in it, but I sat anyway. She smiled. "Now," she said, "tell me everything."

What do you say to a statement like that? I couldn't think of a thing, not one thing. I just sat there on the edge of the chair trying not to get it dirty and carefully not smiling so she wouldn't be shocked by my braces.

"How was your mother when you left her?"

"Fine, thank you."

"She's had a trying time." She gave a little sigh. "I hope it will all work out for her."

What had been trying? Maybe she meant me. I had this sudden feeling that what had been wrong might have been the problems of raising me. But that was crazy! I wasn't *that* bad. And who said anything was wrong?

"Let's hope they will decide to omit the Mexican part of the trip." She wasn't looking at me, and I had the feeling she'd forgotten for a moment that I was there.

"Mexico? They've gone to Europe."

She looked straight at me, a long searching look. She had big dark brown eyes that made you feel as if you were sinking if you looked at them too long. Finally she said, "Oh, your mother mentioned a stop in Mexico later." She got up. "You'd probably like to take a bath and get settled a bit before dinner." She walked out into the hall, leaning a little on that fancy cane. "Your room is the first one on the right. Forgive me if I don't take you up. I broke my hip last year and it's a bit of a bother still, on the stairs."

27

"I didn't know you broke your hip."

"I didn't want to worry your mother with it. She had enough . . ." She broke off. "It healed beautifully. Can you manage your bags?"

"Yes, ma'am." I'd never said "ma'am" in my life before, but it sounded kind of western.

"Oliver should have taken them up for you."

"Is that boy an Indian?"

"Yes. He's a lovely boy."

He hadn't seemed too lovely to me but I didn't say so. "Is his last name really . . . what he said it was?"

"Everybodylooksat. Yes."

"That's a real name?"

"Indians often have picturesque names."

"Does he work for you?"

"Yes. He's trying to get enough money to go to college next year."

I hoisted one of my bags under my arm and picked up the others and hung the tape recorder strap around my neck. "I didn't know Indians went to college."

She gave me that long look again. You could tell I was turning out to be quite a shock to her. "My dear child, you have a lot to learn."

"Sans doute."

She laughed. "The bathroom for your room is right next door to it. We'll have dinner in about forty minutes." She went off somewhere—to the kitchen probably, because I can smell something cooking. In spite of all that food this morning, I am famished. I can't figure out whether what I smell is roast lamb or roast pork. Either way, I don't know if I can stand to wait forty minutes.

I'm trying to get all this stuff recorded before I forget a single thing, before I've even unpacked.

My room is huge, with a four-poster bed and a canopy, like something in a restored historic shrine. There are a couple of books on the bedside table. *Green Mansions* and *My Friend Flicka*. She has to be kidding. I wonder if she realizes how old I am. Old people lose track of time, they say. Although she didn't seem all that old, to tell the truth.

FOUR

I UNPACKED MY STUFF and took a bath in this wild bathtub that stands on metal claws. The plumbing is about 1876, with ornamented silver handles for water faucets and all that, but everything seems to work.

I couldn't decide what to wear to dinner. I didn't want to seem barbaric. I ended up with a denim skirt and a white shirt, and I put on my gunbelt, not to wear to dinner, of course (even I am not that stupid), but just to feel more at home for a few minutes. I sneaked out into the hall to look around. I could hear the sounds of pots and pans from downstairs somewhere. I decided to walk down the long hall. After all, if I am going to live here, I can walk down the hall, I should hope.

There are four bedrooms that look unused, and then a gigantic bedroom with a little dressing room that is obviously my grandmother's. It has a four-poster, too, and a fireplace. I've always wanted a bedroom with a fireplace. Fat chance I'll ever get one. All the rooms are depressingly tidy; I will have to watch my step. It's going to be worse than being at home.

Across the hall and down a little from my room there is a kind of den or something. The wall I can see from the doorway is lined with books, floor to ceiling, and it has a fireplace, too. I thought maybe there would be something jazzier than *Girl of the Limberlost* in there. I looked up and down the corridor to make sure the coast was clear, and then I stepped inside. I nearly screamed. Right there beside me, hanging on the wall, was this gigantic animal. Just his head, fortunately. Stuffed, I guess, but it did give me a turn. It has tremendous antlers but it doesn't look like any deer I ever saw a picture of. It has a big bulgy nose and a hunk of skin and hair hanging from its throat. It is one ugly critter. I suppose its eyes must be fake—like big buttons or something—but they look real. The whole thing gives me the creeps. It's kind of like the wax museum we went to once in St. Augustine, the only time the three of us ever took a trip together. There were all those people that you knew had to be unreal because they'd been dead for a century or two, but there they were, right beside you, looking right at you. I got sick to my stomach and had to be dragged out of there by my father. I remember he said to my mother, "We should either travel a lot more with this child, or not at all." And my mother said, "I told you it would be like this."

I tried to ignore the animal on the wall, though that isn't easy. You have the feeling he is right behind you ready to pounce. I looked at a big rack full of guns. This must have been my grandfather's study. At least I

31

couldn't picture my grandmother out shooting big game. There was a rolltop desk, closed, and a swivel chair, which I sat in and swivelled.

The books in the bookcase weren't too encouraging. There were about twenty books on raising sheep and swine, and the diseases of cattle; and a bunch of books on hunting and fishing. There was a set of Dickens and a very old set of the Encyclopaedia Britannica. I had just picked up a book about guns when I heard my grandmother calling me. I stuck the book back and ran, feeling as if I'd been caught shoplifting. It wasn't till I got to the bottom of the stairs and saw her looking at me that I remembered I had forgotten to take off my gunbelt.

She didn't mention it and I didn't either, so I ate my first meal in my grandmother's house with my gunbelt on, which would have sent my mother into a three-day screaming fit if she had known it. Grandmother had changed into a dress.

On the kitchen table there was a martini pitcher with some ice melting on the bottom, a glass, a bottle of gin, a lemon with some of the peel sliced off, and a bottle of dry vermouth. She saw me looking at them, but she didn't say anything. I guess she figures if she doesn't make me explain about the gunbelt, she shouldn't have to explain about the martinis. Anyway it is nothing to me. My mother can't wait for four o'clock to have her first bourbon. She's not a lush or anything, but she likes two or three bourbons before dinner, and it makes her a lot easier to get along with. There was a time there when Uncle George used to join her for the happy hour, when my father was away on his trips and sometimes at first when he was home, but recently all that stopped. Uncle

George is not my uncle, he's my godfather and a very old friend of my parents. I think the story is that my father met my mother while she was on a date with Uncle George. I never could get terribly interested in all that ancient romance.

Two things I found out during my first evening in Montana: one, my grandmother has a thing about ritual, and two, she is a fantastic cook. One of the rituals is the way dinner is served. Linen tablecloth, the good silver, lighted candles, and a bottle of wine chilling in a silver ice bucket. I thought maybe she was celebrating my arrival but she said she always eats like that, even when she's alone. "Ceremony," she said, "is one of the things one hangs onto—it's one of the ways of reminding yourself you're civilized."

And let me tell you about the food. Roast lamb with a whole bunch of herbs (she grows her own). Banana salad sprinkled with lemon juice and paprika and a cream dressing (I mean real cream from cows) with capers in it. She was pleased that I liked the food, so she gave me a play-by-play description. Potatoes cut up to look like little melon balls, browned in butter. Strawberry shortcake with real homemade shortcake and real whipped cream. Need I say more?

I had been worrying about what to talk to her about, especially at mealtimes when you have to sit there staring at each other, but that problem was solved. We could talk about food.

Then we got on to the unpleasant subject of school. It starts on Monday. It was something I really didn't want to talk about—it is too horrible to contemplate. To change the subject I told her I stayed at the St. Regis, and that was good for about fifteen minutes of reminiscence. She was kind of quiet for a little while after that, and she had another glass of wine.

She kind of shook herself out of the mood and said, "I put some books in your room. I don't know whether you've read them?"

"Thank you very much."

"What kind of books do you like? Maybe those are a little young for you. It's a long time since I've thought about young girls and what they like . . ."

I wasn't trying to be smart. I just said the first thing that came into my head, which happened to be true. "The last book I read was *Portnoy's Complaint*."

"*Portnoy's Complaint?*" Her voice sounded kind of faint.

I couldn't tell if she was surprised or just wasn't familiar with the book. "It was quite funny. It's about . . ."

She put her napkin down and got up, very fast, all in one continuous motion. "I know what it's about. I read the reviews. I usually have my coffee in the living room. Would you like some more milk or something?"

"No, thank you." My right gun banged against the table as I got up, and she looked pained for a moment. It was an antique table with a whole lot of inlay.

She carried a silver tray with a pretty little silver coffee pot and sugar and creamer and a cup that I hoped I'd never have to use because I would break it first thing. She put them on the coffee table and sat down on the white divan. She poured herself a cup of coffee. Cream and sugar. Boy! This is the Wild West? She lit a cigarette.

"Smoking is hazardous to health," I said. I thought

34

maybe living way off here she might not have kept up on these things.

"I'm sure it is, but at my age one doesn't worry too much about that. But you're right, young people shouldn't smoke. It's a stupid habit." She looked at the end of her cigarette. "But it's gotten me through a lot of bad times. To each generation its own vices, I guess. Things change so, and one doesn't always keep up."

"Change is the first rule of life," I said. I am rather fond of statements like that.

She nodded. "So they keep saying. Have you read Heraclitus?" She didn't wait for me to say yes or no, which was fortunate because I never heard of him. "It seems to me change is sort of egg-shaped. And we don't sustain the full shock of it until we're on the diminishing end of the egg."

She'd lost me there so I just said, "Yes, ma'am."

She had lighted the fire in the fireplace before she sat down, and now she just stared at the flames. I think she had forgotten I was there. I cleared my throat, but she didn't move.

Then the telephone rang, and she jumped. I could tell she was a little annoyed at having to answer the phone before the cigarette–coffee ritual was over. The phone is in the study next to the living room. I could hear her saying, "Hello? . . . Hello? . . . I can't hear you . . ." Pause. "The connection is bad. I can't . . . Cassandra, is that you?"

Nobody calls my mother Cassandra but that's her name all right. I got all shaky and I didn't know whether to go into the den or stay where I was.

Grandmother was projecting. "Cassandra, dear, how

are you? . . . Wonderful. . . . Oh, yes, she's here. Nothing to worry about." Long pause. "Well, it's very interesting to meet my only grandchild after all these years."

Interesting!

"Yes, we're getting acquainted. It's a little like Act One, Scene One; we're just feeling our way through the exposition. But tell me about your trip." Long pause. "Of course. Fine. She's right here. Marianne? It's your mother."

I tripped over a footstool but no serious damage. "Mother?" There went that squeak in my voice.

"Marianne, honey, how are you?" She sounded amazingly near.

"Fine, thank you, how are you?" What a conversation —and at transatlantic rates!

"How do you like Montana?" Something was odd about her voice. Almost as if she were trying not to cry.

"I don't know yet. Okay, I guess."

"Oh, you'll love it. You'll feel right at home with all those cowboys."

Cowboys! She doesn't even remember what it's like. I haven't seen a cowboy since I got here, except the Indian. "How's Paris?"

"Marvelous. We had dinner at Maxim's and we went to the ballet."

It occurred to me that it must be extremely late in Paris; probably tomorrow, in fact.

"Your father wants to say hello." There was a lot of background noise and voices and then my father said, "Hi there, Tippy." I almost burst into tears right then. It's been years since he called me Tippy.

"Hi," I said. "Are you having fun?"

"Marvelous." He was saying things off the phone, presumably to my mother, and the conversation was a little hard to pursue.

"Are you going to Venice?" I don't know why I asked him that. It was where they'd gone on their honeymoon. They hadn't even mentioned Venice.

He didn't answer for a second, and I thought he hadn't heard me. Then he said, "No, Tippy, I don't think so. Your mother says everything mildews in Venice."

Then my mother came back on and gave me a flock of instructions about picking up my clothes and helping Grandmother, and then she talked to Grandmother again, and it was over. Paris had been right there in the room, and now it was gone.

We went back to the living room. My grandmother looked tired. "What did they say about Venice?"

"Daddy said Mother says everything mildews."

She poured herself some more coffee. Her cigarette had burned down to almost nothing. She threw it into the fireplace and lighted another one. I would have to get her some pamphlets about lung cancer. "Mildew," she said. "Yes, I suppose it does. Nothing is perfect." She looked at me. "You might stow that line away somewhere in your mind for future reference. Nothing is perfect."

"Right on," I said. That's one of my favorite phrases. Also "up against the wall," although it's hard to find occasion for saying that.

Remembering what my mother had said about helping, I offered to wash the dishes but she said no, thank you, she had a dishwasher. That was jake with me.

"One thing you'll discover about me," she said, "is

that I am rather a fanatic about schedule. I like to do the same things at pretty much the same time every day. For instance, I go for a ride before breakfast."

"Ride?" I thought of the old Chevrolet.

"Yes. I have two quite splendid horses, a lovely little Morgan mare and a bay gelding. You'll enjoy the mare. She's a bit skittish till she gets to know you, but she's really a love."

If there is one thing I'm more afraid of than water, it's a horse. My father took me riding in Fenway Park six different times, and I was thrown six different times. The last time, the horse came back and stepped on my foot. During my one ill-fated summer at a girls' camp, I made my team lose the All-Season Award because I refused to get on a horse.

When I didn't say anything, she said, "Perhaps tomorrow you'll be a little tired. Would you prefer to wait?"

"Yes, ma'am."

She raised her eyebrows. "You don't really have to call me ma'am, you know." She studied me. "Do you find it hard to call me Grandmother?"

"Yes'm."

"Well, there's no rule about it. Call me whatever you like."

"What else is there?" I said. Grandma and Gran and Nana were obviously out of the question.

She shrugged. "Call me Katherine, if you like."

I was shocked. "I couldn't do that."

She laughed. "Mrs. Carter?" She stood looking down at me, amused. There's nothing that makes me more uneasy than that. You keep thinking: what's funny? What did I do now? "One of my other habits," she said, "is to go to bed early and read late. If you hear me wandering around the house at two or three in the morning, don't be alarmed. I'm an insomniac."

She brushed a piece of hair off my forehead. "See you in the morning then. Breakfast is at seven."

Seven! I can't even get both eyes open before ten. And before I recovered from that shock, I happened to look at her hand. She was looking at it, too. There were black streaks on her fingers. My hair tint.

I mumbled good night and bolted upstairs. I locked myself in the bathroom and washed my hair for about thirty-five minutes. It's almost back to normal, only kind of streaked.

My sheets are pink, with flowers. This is not the true West at all. I've been sold a bill of goods.

FIVE

SHE WOKE ME UP THIS MORNING. I vaguely remembered that my alarm clock had rung and I'd turned it off. "Breakfast in fifteen minutes," she said. I had one eye half open, but even with that limited vision I could see this picture of glowing health and energy standing beside my bed. It was depressing. Her cheeks were red and her hair was kind of blown and her eyes sparkled. Dear God. I managed a sitting position and the damp towel fell off my head.

She picked it up. "I hope you won't catch cold. Let me know next time; I have a dryer. I like to do my own hair."

Of course, she would have a dryer. With all this civilization I'd expected her to be wearing pinks for her morning ride or something, but there she was in blue jeans and a red sweater.

By the time I staggered downstairs to breakfast, she

40

was bringing to the table orange juice and fried eggs and ham and baking powder biscuits with blueberry preserves. At least this visit was going to be a gastronomic success.

"Did you have a good ride?" That was the only thing I could think of to say, but it worked pretty well. For several minutes she talked about how pretty the woods were. Red sumac, green evergreens, golden tamarack . . . I made appropriate murmurs from time to time. Finally she stopped.

It was obvious that I was expected to say something. I looked at her groggily. "I'm not very interesting early in the morning." That wasn't quite what I'd meant to say.

But she smiled and said, "My husband used to quote Oscar Wilde: 'Only dull people are brilliant at breakfast.' "

"What was he like?" I've discovered that sometimes a well-placed question can let you off the conversational hook for quite a while.

"Oscar Wilde?"

"No, your husband." It's funny how neither of us ever referred to him as my grandfather. I never really thought of myself as having a grandfather, not having had one since the age of one.

She looked kind of dreamily out the window. "That would take a lot of telling. He was quite a man."

Big deal. Now I knew him inside out.

"He was compelling enough to make me give up everything I loved most—the theater, New York, my friends and family." She went into a reverie.

I wanted to ask her if he was compelling enough to make her glad she'd done it, but I didn't.

It turned out that during the morning Katherine cleans house and then she disappears into her study. I don't know what she does there. I went out and wandered around.

There was a big yard with big old droopy trees—willows, I guess—and a hammock thing under the trees. Then there was a barn, which I went into with due caution. It was empty. It had three stalls, and there was a bunch of tack hanging on the wall. (Tack is a word I picked up during my six rides in Fenway Park.) The whole place was almost as neat and clean as the house. It smelled horsey but kind of pleasant. I looked out a little window at the back of the barn, and I nearly dropped dead. There was a huge big horse looking right back at me, his face right up to the window. Once I realized that he couldn't stomp on me through the barn wall, I regained my poise. Actually he had a pretty face, with a white blaze from his forehead to his nose.

"Ha ha ha," I said to him. "You can't tromp on me."

"He wouldn't tromp on you."

I whirled around, and there was the redskin. I hadn't even heard him come in. James Fenimore Cooper was right about the stealthy tread. "I was just soliloquizing," I said, as loftily as possible. It's demoralizing to be caught talking out loud when nobody's there.

"That's okay. I talk to animals all the time. I just said he wouldn't tromp you, at least not on purpose. Cyrano is a good horse."

"Cyrano?"

"Yeah. The mare is down at the other end of the corral. You'll be riding her."

"I don't think so."

"How come?" He wanted to know.

"I have a back injury." I didn't want to get any further into that, so I went back to the house and did this taping.

Here's a major catastrophe! There's no TV. No TV in the whole house. There are two stereos, one in Katherine's study and one in her bedroom, with stacks of records, mostly opera and symphonies and things—no hard rock that I could discover. In the kitchen there's a little radio but she shuts it off right after the weather report. The daily paper is mostly about what the Daughters of Job are doing and what the price of hogs is. What am I going to *do?* Farewell to *Gunsmoke*—farewell, Virginian—goodbye, Hoss. I'm cut off from the whole world.

After lunch Katherine walks. She took me along with her, and after five minutes I realized what a mistake I had made in wearing my boots. They hurt. Walking with Katherine is like taking a stroll with Artemis, the goddess of the hunt (I think it's Artemis). She has long legs; even with that little limp and the cane, she strides across the face of the earth. I'm not sure she needs the cane. I do not have long legs and I have an unfortunate tendency to stub my toe.

Finally, when I could hardly bear to put one foot down after the other, she stopped. "It's beautiful, isn't it," she said. She wasn't even breathing hard.

"What?"

She looked a little puzzled. "Why, the woods. Autumn. All of it."

"Oh," I said, "it sure is." Actually I hadn't had time to look up. I stumbled over to a vacant tree trunk and sat

43

down. It really *was* pretty. Some of the trees were green, being evergreens, and some were gold, and you could see the mountains with snow on their tops.

"Why are you limping?" she asked.

"I seem to have a blister on my heel. On both heels, as a matter of fact."

"Oh. It's not a good idea to walk in boots; I should have noticed. Do you have any sneakers?"

"No."

"We'll get you some. We'd better cut short our walk if your feet hurt."

Cut it short! We'd already covered half of Montana.

"The boots will be good for riding, of course."

I had to break it to her sometime. "I'm afraid I'm not going to be able to ride."

"Oh?"

"I have this back condition."

"What kind of back condition?"

"Well, sort of like calcium deposits. The doctor said it would be fatal to be on a horse. I might end up with a split disc."

She looked at me closely. "Calcium? At your age?"

"Well, when it comes to disease, I'm old for my years." I could tell she didn't believe a word of it, but she let it go.

After we got home, she looked at my blisters. They were impressive. When she had sprayed them with some cool stuff and put bandaids on them, she traced my foot on a piece of paper, and then she called Oliver, who was doing something with hay.

"Ollie, will you go to Pearson's and get Marianne a pair of sneakers? This is her foot size."

"Right," he said.

But when Oliver came back, he had beautiful chocolate-colored squaw boots. At least he called them squaw boots. They were moccasins, only ankle high, with a top that folded over and was fringed. There were a few beads on the fronts. They were marvelous.

"Didn't they have sneakers?" Katherine asked.

"Yes, but they were hideous."

I thought it was nice that he didn't want me to wear hideous sneakers.

"I like these," I said.

"Squaw boots are comfortable," Katherine said, "except when you step on something sharp."

"Is she a tenderfoot?" Oliver grinned.

"I'm sure they'll be just fine," I said. Just to show him, I walked outside and immediately stepped on a few sharp pebbles and had to lunge to get off them. Katherine and Oliver were watching, so I pretended that I was doing a little high-spirited dance. They laughed.

SIX

I HAVE WAITED TWO WEEKS to tape my first experiences with school. They have been too hideous to contemplate any more than was absolutely necessary.

The school house was built in 1914, and it smells of wet rubbers even on a dry day. The desks are so carved up with initials, you can't put down a piece of paper and write on it without its getting full of holes. It's kind of weird to think that a lot of the people who belong to those initials are grown up or old or even dead.

In the sophomore class there are nine kids, of whom I am one. Our teacher is waiting for retirement, and she's not waiting with any grace. She teaches us algebra, which I've already had, and French, which I've had since fifth grade, and social studies, which is a hodgepodge of nothing. The junior and senior classes meet with us for social studies. For English they meet with us, too, and we have a different teacher, who is younger and nicer.

English isn't too bad.

In the sophomore class there are four Indian kids, who are quite nice but shy and they hang together, and four girls, whom I will call A, B, C and D, because I do not wish to distinguish them with names. A is tall and skinny, B is tall and plump, C is short and skinny, and D is beautiful. All of them have hideous personalities, and they hate me. They started making fun of me the minute I entered the school, and they will probably never quit.

In the English class there are some big boys, including Oliver. He graduated last year, but he's reviewing English because it's his worst subject. There is also a big bully named Patrick, who is the son of the assistant sheriff. He's so big, he sprawls all over the aisle, and he's proud of the fact that he's completely ignorant. Oliver says nothing at all unless he's called on, and then he usually knows the answer. Oliver has a little half brother named Dougie Three-Toes, who's about seven, and Dougie hangs around the school when Oliver is there. Patrick tried to tease Dougie the other day, and Oliver nearly beat him up. At least he talked very tough.

Anyway, these girls, A, B, C and D, think it's hilarious that I wear boots and jeans and things. They ware revolting miniskirts; they haven't even heard that miniskirts are out of style. I told them. They call me the dude, and they're always asking me if I want to go on a pack trip or something.

They keep asking me to ride with them, because I happened to tell them that I ride English—which I did —and they think I can't ride western—which I can't.

I have tried various methods of stalling them off, like ignoring them, which isn't easy, or taking a lofty tone, that makes them laugh like fiends, or getting mad, which they love. It is a trying situation, and I don't know where it will all end.

Katherine is going away tomorrow for three days, to Helena. She has three friends that play bridge with her Saturday nights. One of them is a retired doctor, Dr. Goodwin, quite ancient—about eighty, I think—although he has all his faculties all right. And another man, not quite so old, who is a retired rancher, named Mr. Bartlett. And the young doctor who is taking Dr. Goodwin's place. Mr. Bartlett and Dr. Goodwin are widowers, and Dr. Francis Wilson is single and about thirty-five. Apparently Katherine and her husband chummed around with the Bartletts and the Goodwins in the old days. They reminisce a lot, which must bore the young doctor, but he doesn't act bored. When they aren't playing bridge, they talk about what the *New York Times* (which arrives six days late) said about the newest plays, and they swap new books around and all that. Dr. Goodwin tries to get me into the conversation by asking me questions when he's doing the Double Acrostic in Katherine's *Saturday Review*. "Marianne," he'll say, "who was the first ruler in the Second Angevin Dynasty? Five letters."

And if I say, "What's an Angevin Dynasty?" they laugh as if I'm the world's greatest wit. What *is* an Angevin Dynasty?

I usually sit in a corner and pretend to read, because being there isn't quite as lonesome as being upstairs by myself. And besides, there's the fondue. At eleven sharp, Katherine whips up a fondue, and it's worth sitting there all evening being bored.

48

But I digress. Katherine is going to Helena with Dr. Francis and Dr. Goodwin to the governor's ball. They are buddies of the governor. I will be looked after by Oliver's aunt, that he and Dougie live with—Mrs. Foxtail, whom I like very much. She is fat and good-natured and she has no discernible teeth. And she doesn't care what I do so long as I don't kill myself. She cleans house for Katherine two days a week. Oliver and Dougie may stay here too, while Katherine is gone. It will be a change. Oliver and his family are Kootenai Indians, by the way. And I asked him what the wooden sidewalk on the main street is for (he was in one of his good moods at the time). It's because the snow gets so deep, they have to build the sidewalk up high to keep it clear of snow.

SEVEN

I AM IN GRAVE DANGER. Today at school I lost my
head and I bragged about what a great horsewoman I am
back East. I told them I ride to the hounds and all that.
D challenged me to ride with them this afternoon. When
I tried to get out of it, she said I was a liar and a coward.
I *am* a liar and a coward; why didn't I just agree with her
and go home? But no, I had to play Joan of Arc. The
result: we set forth on a riding expedition in fifteen
minutes. This may be my last recording. But honor
must be preserved.

EIGHT

I PUT ON MY JODHPURS and my black velvet hunting cap that my father got me when he still had hopes I'd be a horsewoman. I brought them with me because I like to wear them around the house, though the pants are getting very tight. (Were, I should say.)

To relate this story is very painful, even to my only true friend, the tape recorder.

I asked Oliver to saddle Candida.

He looked surprised. "I thought you had a bad back."

"Don't argue," I said. "I have accepted a challenge."

He said, "If you mean those stupid girls at school, forget it. They're no challenge to anybody but their mothers."

"My honor is at stake."

"Oh, don't be stupid."

"If you don't saddle Candida, I'll ride her bareback."

Boy, was that a bluff!

"If your grandmother was here, she wouldn't let you go."

"She would, too. She'd help me uphold the family honor."

Grumbling he got the saddle and put it on. "You'll fall off, and I'll get blamed." He tried to boost me into the saddle, but I have very short legs. Finally he got a box, and I stood on it, and he heaved me onto the horse. I almost fell off on the other side, but he grabbed my foot.

"This is insane," he said. He helped me get the reins straight; western reins aren't like eastern reins. And the saddle has a horn that one could easily impale himself on. On the other hand, you can hang onto it if you're in deep trouble. As I found out. "She's got a sensitive mouth," he said. "Don't saw on the reins. Neck-rein her. And try not to do anything idiotic."

"Oh, don't be so superior." I rode out of the yard with dignity, wondering what neck-rein meant. I walked the horse to the canyon to meet the four witches, but just when we came in sight of them, Candida decided to trot. That was the first of many misfortunes. I have been taught the rudiments of posting, so I tried to post. It seems you don't post on a western horse. Every time I came down, Candida went up, and vice versa. The four witches nearly fell off their horses laughing. I tried to say, "What's so funny?" but it came out very joggled. Luckily Candida stopped to greet the other horses.

"That hat!" B screamed. "What's that hat?"

"It happens to be regulation for eastern riding." I tried to sound in full command, but it wasn't coming off.

"Well, let's go." D kicked her horse in the ribs, and he flew up in the gravel road with the others right behind him. Candida, not wishing to be left behind, also flew. If there hadn't been that little rise in the back of the saddle, I'd have been left on the ground.

By the time we reached the first curve in the road, I had dropped the reins and was hanging onto the saddle horn with both hands. When Candida stopped behind the others, I nearly flew over her head.

"Maybe we should quit," A said. "She might get hurt." A actually proved to be slightly humanitarian.

"Quit nothing," said D. "She's done all this fancy bragging about her damned dude riding. Let her show us." And she charged on up the hill.

Candida followed, and, in spite of Oliver's instructions, I grabbed at the reins and sawed. Candida threw up her head. Then she reared. The others were out of sight. I dropped the reins and tried to grab the horn but she reared again, and I was dumped right in the middle of the road. Candida turned around and lit out for home.

Nothing was broken, but I hurt all over. I sat there for a minute, trying not to cry. I couldn't help remembering I'd got myself into this. Then I heard hooves coming down the hill. I was damned if I would let them find me there like a sack of potatoes. Although it was very painful, I got up. I thought of hiding in the brush until they'd gone by, but that seemed craven. I moved to the side of the road and suddenly I had a sickening realization. The whole back seam of my jodhpurs had ripped out!

I stood with my back to the bushes when they came up.

"Hey," D said, "where's your horse?"

I looked past them as if there were something very fascinating on the other side of the road. "Home, I presume."

They were grinning from ear to ear. Although A said, "You aren't hurt, are you?" Her name is Alice, and she's not as bad as the others.

"Certainly not."

"Can you make it home?"

I was terrified that they would see my torn pants. That would have been the ultimate humiliation.

"Naturally."

"Well, I was just trying to be humane." She was annoyed now. The milk of human kindness curdles quickly.

"Listen," D said, "why worry about her? She's the big flash from the East. She doesn't need any help from us." She has a habit of starting her horse very fast from a standstill, like a kid vrooming his car off from a traffic light. I got a faceful of gravel as she took off. The others followed her.

Obviously I couldn't go home until after dark. I couldn't walk through town with the whole back of my pants gone. I sat down on some moss. Pride goeth before a fall all right. Since nobody was around, I cried for a few minutes.

I'd never been in the woods alone before. I was scared. And I knew it would get worse when it grew dark. I kept looking over my shoulder at the trees behind me. They were very thick and dark. I thought about bears. And mountain lions. Coyotes. Wolves. When they tell you how great the West is, they don't mention how it feels to be alone in the forest with wild animals and no seat to your pants.

It was unbelievable that my parents could have abandoned me to this savage land. I cried some more.

Finally I heard a car, and I didn't know whether to be glad or alarmed. I tried to look as though I'd just sat down on the moss because it was a nice place to sit. I examined a leaf very carefully, not looking up when the car got close.

It stopped. "What's wrong?" It was Oliver.

I was so relieved, I could hardly stand it.

"Are you all right? Candida came home."

"Yes."

"Well, get in the car."

I couldn't look him in the face. "I can't stand up."

"Why not?" He sounded scared. "Are you hurt?"

"No."

"Then get in the car." Now he was just mad. "I *told* you not to go."

There was no way out of telling him. "My pants are split."

"Oh, is that all." He took off his sweater and threw it to me. He didn't look at me again. I felt like a fool. "It could have happened to anybody," I said.

He didn't say anything on the way home. Dougie and Mrs. Foxtail met me at the door. They looked concerned, but they didn't ask any questions. Some Indians are nice. I wonder if it would be possible for me to live on an Indian reservation.

Now I have had a bath and daubed my cuts and bruises with iodine, and Dougie has just knocked at my door to say dinner is ready. I had considered fasting, as penance for my false pride, and also because I am sick of Oliver's smug face, but I am quite hungry and something smells wonderful. I believe I will go down. Later I will try to think of some plan for coping with my predicament.

NINE

I HAVE DISCOVERED NATURE. And it's not all its cracked up to be.

Last night, extending the olive branch, Oliver asked me if I wanted to go on a hike in the woods with Dougie and him. He's doing some kind of investigation for the Forest Service, about elk. I would have preferred to stay in my room all day because my bones hurt and so did my soul, but when someone is determined to cheer you up, how can you say no? I did not discover until after I accepted that we were to leave at *five o'clock in the morning!!*

Actually I woke up at four and I was ready for half an hour before Dougie knocked on my door.

It was still dark, and the thermometer said thirty-one. Mrs. Foxtail was up and had already fixed us pancakes and coffee. At home in Boston I don't drink coffee. I don't really like it, but I like the idea.

I wore the down-filled parka that I'd bought for winter, and wool socks and my squaw boots. I felt like a real Indian. With the socks on, it didn't hurt so much when I stepped on pebbles and things.

We drove about ten miles in the Chevrolet, and then we left it and started walking through woods with very tall trees. It was still dark but there was a gray streak down low on the horizon, like a reflection, as if somebody had left a light on. The birds were singing like maniacs. In Boston you don't have much in the way of birds except robins and pigeons, or if you do, I've never noticed them. Once we stopped and looked at a kind of swampy place with tall weeds that were full of birds. Oliver said they were red-winged blackbirds.

I told him he must be wrong. They looked completely black to me.

"Watch carefully," he said. "Watch when they make that cheeping noise."

It's maddening, the way he's always right. When they cheeped, their chests sort of heaved up and their wings lifted a little, and you could see real scarlet. Then three of them took off at once, and it was like three little flames streaking through the air. I'm going to get a bird book at Mr. Pearson's store. I had no idea.

Dougie was carrying a fishing pole and pretty soon we were walking along a river that was full of rocks. I kept turning my ankle. You could see the sun just showing red above the skyline now. It was the first time I ever saw the sunrise outdoors. Sometimes when I can't sleep at home, I see it come up kind of dirty and pale over the old brick buildings of Boston. This was something else. You felt like breathing deep. In fact, I did.

58

We sat down beside the river for a little while and ate a bunch of popcorn that Oliver had in the little pack on his back. Dougie tapped my arm and pointed to the other side of the river, a little way upstream. There was this animal! He was brown and furry and about three feet long. I shrieked. He slid off the bunch of sticks he was on and slapped the water with his tail and disappeared. "What was it?" I said.

Oliver shook his head, as if he'd never encountered such ignorance.

"Beaver," Dougie said.

Dougie took me by the hand, and we went up to the place where the beaver had disappeared, although I was scared. I asked Dougie if they would bite, and he laughed. He has very black eyes and a round face and he laughs more than he talks.

He pointed to a kind of cone-shaped thing made of sticks. "Beavers make dams."

It was fantastic, how that thing was built. I forgot about being scared of the beaver, and I got down on my stomach to look at it. It looks like something people would build. Just above it was the little pool it had dammed off. Dougie put an icky sickening worm on his fishhook and dropped the line into the pool. Nothing happened. I don't think I'd like fishing; you have to wait too long.

I went back to sit beside Oliver. He was making notes on a clipboard, but they weren't very interesting. Something about exactly where we were, what the wind direction was, and stuff like that. He didn't like my looking over his shoulder.

Just when we were ready to go, there was a big splash

and Dougie had a fish on his line. It leaped up out of the water and hit again. It looked awfully big, and Dougie had to fight to hang onto the rod.

"Help him," I said, but Oliver shook his head.

"He'd never forgive me."

It took about five minutes before he got the fish onto the bank, where it flopped like mad. Oliver said it was a cutthroat trout. He picked it up right by the gills and showed me the red stripe under its jaw. I felt terrible for the poor fish. And then a really ghastly thing happened. Dougie picked up a rock and hit the trout on the back of the head and killed him. I couldn't believe it.

"You shouldn't do such a thing," I said. "That's murder."

Dougie looked at me as if I had gone crazy, but he was too happy with his fish to worry much about me.

"Come on," Oliver said. "We'll be back after a while, Dougie."

"O.K." Dougie put the fish in the water and weighted it down with a rock.

"That's awful," I said. "That poor fish."

Oliver shrugged. "We have to eat."

"But you should buy . . ." I stopped, and he grinned.

"Buy our fish at the store?"

Of course, I got the point but I still felt sick. "I never thought about it before."

"We're part of nature like everything else. What did you think you were—something special?" He gave me a hand across the stream on a bunch of stones. They were wet and slippery and I could feel the icy water slosh into my boots. The water was moving fast and it made me dizzy although it wasn't deep. I really am a coward about water. "You're part of the food chain."

I thought about it for a while. I couldn't talk anyway because we were climbing a little hill and I was out of breath. When we got to the top, I said, "Yes, but nobody eats man."

"When a man dies, his body nourishes the earth."

I didn't find it too jolly a line of thought so I gave it up. Maybe Indians have a different outlook on life. My feet were squishy wet and cold, and I was hungry again. I wanted to go home. The sun was up now, though, and I hoped maybe it would get warmer. We went over the top of the hill and down the other side into a meadow. Oliver had to stop to make some more notes, stuff about sedge grass and all. I was getting bored with all this note-taking. And Nature can be quite cold and uncomfortable. The meadow was pretty—full of tall frizzy purple flowers that Oliver said were bull thistle.

On the other side of the meadow there was a little lake. He picked out a clump of trees and told me to lie down and be quiet. He can be very bossy. It wasn't too charming lying there on the ground, with the root of a pine tree sticking into my stomach, but whenever I even breathed he gave me a dirty look.

It seemed to me that he was planning for us to spend the rest of our lives there, and I was getting really sick of it. I was just about to say so when he pointed. At first I couldn't see anything, but then this beautiful, *really* beautiful deer stepped out of the trees and went down to the water and began to drink. It was so beautiful, I felt like fainting. Then another one came. The second one had *antlers!* Both of them had big ears, and they were kind of reddish-brown. I had never seen a live deer before in my whole life. I was so excited, I didn't think I could stand it. I guess I wiggled around a little because the one with the antlers shot his head up in the air and gave a little baaa, like a sheep, and the two of them took off, leaping like something out of the ballet. It was almost too much to endure.

"Lie still," Oliver whispered.

Nothing happened for a while, and then a dark brown creature waddled down to the water, heavy and on short legs. I poked Oliver to find out what it was and he wrote "woodchuck" on his pad.

Suddenly the woodchuck scuttled off, as if he'd been scared. And then I heard a crashing in the woods, and *I* was scared. I clutched Oliver's arm but he shook me off. Three absolutely gigantic creatures came out of the trees and went down to drink. They looked like the deer only much bigger and there was something different about the antlers, bigger and narrower. "Elk," Oliver wrote on his pad.

Elk! In one little piece of a morning I had seen red-winged blackbirds, beaver, deer, woodchuck, elk! And I hadn't thought of the four witches one minute.

Oliver was writing away on his pad. I wondered if my mother knew about all this. She had been born in Montana, but according to her stories, she spent a lot of time in Europe and in the East at various schools. She never had much to say about Montana. I had to admit it had its good points, even though I was shivering and hungry.

After the elk had gone, Oliver measured their footprints and wrote the figures down. Then he showed me a bunch of other prints and told me what they all were. Skunk, mink, weasel, fox, rabbit—it was astonishing how

62

he could tell them all. I found one that looked like a people track, but he said it was a possum. They have opposable thumbs, like us!

At last he said we had to go back because he had work to do at home. It was okay with me. When we got to Dougie, he had six more fish, none of them as big as the first one. I tried not to look at them—they looked so dead. But when we got home, Mrs. Foxtail cooked some of them, and although at first I refused to eat them, hunger overcame my scruples, and I have to admit I never tasted anything so good.

Oliver says I can go out with him again tomorrow if I'll be quiet. Gad! if I was any quieter, I'd be dead.

TEN

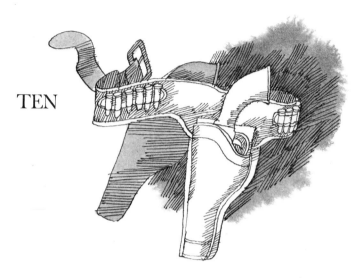

Fisher: eats squirrels, mice, raccoons, vegetables, rabbits. Also *porcupines!*

3 Painted Turtles: eat plants, insects, shellfish if handy, unborn mosquitoes, dead animals that happen along.

Track of bobcat: looks like a hand. Eats rabbits, birds, mice.

Trees with bark chewed off: indicating porcupine. Eats: bark, leaves, twigs.

Osprey: kinky wings, otherwise looks like an eagle. Eats fish.

Meadowlark: sings like the angels. Eats bugs, grain.

Purple finch: looks like a sparrow that fell into a pot of raspberry jam. Eats bugs.

* * *

Two really outstanding things today. First, Oliver told me one of his most secret secrets. Out on an island in a lake somewhere he is taking care of an osprey that was shot in one wing and can't fly. He feeds him. The osprey has gotten very tame and follows him around, he says, "Like an old hen." I didn't dare ask if I could see it, but he may offer someday. He clams up if you ask too much.

The second thing, and this is almost too fabulous to tell: we were lying in the brush by the watering place again just after dawn watching the gang come down for a drink, and suddenly here was this magnificent big buck and a doe (I know the difference now). Oliver poked me and signalled me to watch. They kept very close together, the doe sort of nudging the buck along, not at all like the other animals. When they finished drinking and turned toward me, I saw the buck's eyes. They were *white!* I mean all white, like milk. After they had gone, Oliver told me the buck is blind and the doe takes him everywhere and looks after him. He's been watching them for two years.

I cried so hard he had to take me home and that made him cross.

One other thing. On the way home, a different way from yesterday, I wanted to get a drink out of the stream and he wouldn't let me. I thought he was being ornery, and I got down on my stomach to drink anyway. He grabbed me by the back of my jacket and hauled me up and pointed out in the water. A big fish was floating along on the current, dead.

"When I say don't drink, don't drink," he said. "This

river is polluted."

I couldn't believe it. So the Charles River in Boston is polluted and the East River in New York and Lake Erie—but *here?*

"There's a logging operation up above. The sediment and the increased water temperature kill the fish and pollute the water."

"Why doesn't somebody stop it?"

He shrugged.

"How can you be so indifferent?" I said, and he gave me a funny look. I told him I was going to write a letter to the paper.

To the Editor:
Dear Sir:

Are you aware that not more than fifteen miles from town the logging operations being carried on by the Northwest Lumber Company are polluting the East Fishhook River? Conservationists, take note! Fishermen, unite! Stop this unholy desecration of our Treasure State's magnificent waterways. ACT BEFORE IT IS TOO LATE.

Signed:
E Pluribus Unum.

After school tomorrow I'll leave it with Mr. Faber at the newspaper. He's a nice man. He saw me peering in the window one day and he invited me in and found out who I was and all.

There was a letter from my mother today—two, in fact—one for me, one for Katherine, who will be home in half an hour or so. Mine sounded funny–peculiar,

66

terribly gay one minute and depressed the next. They are in London, and Uncle George has joined them. That in itself is odd. Although I guess anybody can go to London who wants to. But why does she sound so sad?

Tomorrow I have to go back to school and face the music.

It is about two hours later and Katherine hasn't come. It's getting dark, and Mrs. Foxtail and the boys have gone. I wanted them to stay, and Mrs. Foxtail offered to, but I couldn't admit it because Oliver grinned like a fiend and asked me if I was afraid of the dark. Naturally I had to say I didn't mind being alone at all.

But I do. The wind is howling like somebody in pain, and it's starting to snow. This house is terribly big. I've turned on all the lights, but I am scared. Everything is creaking and banging. There must be a shutter loose, but it sounds like somebody trying to get in. I wish I were home. I'm in Katherine's husband's den because the guns are there. I'd be scared to touch one, but at least they're there. I could say to an intruder, "If you come a step nearer, I'll blow your brains out." I have my gunbelt on but it keeps slipping down over my hips, and when I walk, the guns hit me. I'm going to have to get a new one, but it won't be the same.

That head on the wall is a moose. I looked it up. He stares down at me and if I were not a rational person, I could go out of my mind.

I have brought the radio up here, and I am going to listen to it for a minute, just so I can hear a human voice.

* * *

It was the local news, which goes on for about an hour. The announcer was talking to somebody from the Fish and Game Commission, about how the hunting looks. It looks good, he said. Oliver told me that if they didn't hunt the deer, there would be a deer population explosion and a lot of deer would die of starvation. I don't care what anybody says, I think it's a terrible system, where you have to die to stay alive. I didn't kill you, Moose; you don't have to look at me like that.

I called up the radio station on the phone in Katherine's room and told the announcer I thought it was a terrible system and I am sick of all this killing. He sounded very surprised. He said, "Lady, I didn't invent it." I said I wanted to talk to that Fish and Game man who was urging everybody to go out and kill. He said, "I think you misunderstood him, lady." I said, "Let me talk to him." I am getting a little hysterical. The window panes in Katherine's room are rattling like old bones and the snow is falling everywhere. He said, "I'm sorry, that was a tape." He started to thank me for calling in, and I said, "Don't go. Please don't go." He said, "I have to. I'm the only man on the board." "No," I said, and I was crying. He said, "Lady, are you all right? Do you want me to call the sheriff?" I couldn't say anything, and he said, "I've got to make a station break but I'll be right back." And then he was gone. I hung up.

I thought I heard someone downstairs. I ran back to the study, and my gunbelt slipped down around my knees and nearly tripped me up. I had to take it off.

The radio says there's heavy snow on MacDonald Pass. Katherine may never get here. They might even get killed or freeze to death.

I think there is someone on the stairs. If I turn on the radio again, he may think there is a man here to defend me.

". . . your local radio station, bringing you the time and weather. It's seven fourteen . . . no, make that seven seventeen . . . here in the valley, and the temperature is eighteen degrees above zero. And it's snowing. The Highway Commission warns against travel on Mullan Pass, Rogers Pass and MacDonald Pass. The road to the Park has been closed. Repeat: travel conditions hazardous. And now here's Judy Collins singing *For Everything There Is a Season, Turn, Turn, Turn,* . . ."

"Who is knocking on the door? I have guns here. I will blow your head off. Who is pounding on the door? Go away! I have guns here. I will kill you!"

". . . turn, turn, turn. . . ."

ELEVEN

". . . AND THERE SHE WAS, trying to get Ben's thirty-aught-six down from the wall," Mr. Bartlett said to his housekeeper.

"I thought you were an intruder." I was sitting in a huge leather chair in front of Mr. Bartlett's fireplace, all wrapped up in a blanket that Mrs. Nye, the housekeeper, got me. She is a nice white-haired lady, and she brought me my dinner by the fireplace.

"I called and called to you, but you were yelling at me and the radio was on . . ."

"You're still shivering, honey," Mrs. Nye said. "Do you think you're catching a cold?"

"No." I was shivering because I was still so scared. You don't get unscared all that fast.

"Mrs. Carter and them are all right, are they?" Mrs. Nye said to Mr. Bartlett.

"Oh, they're fine. They're holed up in a motel till the

snow clears. She tried to call you," he said to me, "but the phone was busy."

"I was talking to the radio station."

"Oh. Checking on the storm, were you?" He gave me a nod of approval. "You've got a head on your shoulders, young lady. You'll do all right."

It was so nice to be approved of, I almost forgot it was for the wrong reasons.

"It must seem strange to you, out here in the West," Mrs. Nye said, "growing up back East like you done."

"Oh, I think I've always been a westerner at heart," I said.

Mr. Bartlett chuckled. "Got some of your granddad in you. By George, he'd have been tickled to see you trying to get that gun out of the rack. Regular pioneer woman."

I stopped shivering. I guess I *had* coped rather well, after all. "It just seemed like the rational thing to do," I said.

"What if she'd shot you?" Mrs. Nye said. "By mistake, I mean."

"Oh, lordy, there hasn't been a shell in that gun for years."

I leaned toward him. "You see," I said, "what I figured was, the intruder *wouldn't know that.*"

Mrs. Nye brought me homemade vanilla ice cream with homemade fudge sauce and pecans. It was better than Brigham's back in Boston.

I spent the night at Mr. Bartlett's, in an enormous room in a tremendous bed with a mattress made of feathers. It was an amazing experience. You sink down in this thing like you're lying on marshmallows. I fell asleep before I'd even had time to savor the sensation to the utmost.

In the morning I had sort of a cough, and Mrs. Nye said I'd better stay in bed. She brought me my breakfast in bed and a whole bunch of confession magazines. Boy, they're really something! Talk about *Portnoy's Complaint*.

The sun came out and the wind got very warm, and the snow melted so fast I couldn't believe it. Mrs. Nye said it was a chinook.

In the afternoon Katherine and the men got back, and Mr. Bartlett told her how splendidly I'd handled everything. Katherine is quite proud of me.

Tomorrow, though, I'll have to go back to school.

TWELVE

UNFORTUNATELY my cough disappeared by Tuesday, and I had to go to school. I handled the problem by simply being very aloof. It was obvious that the Four had told everyone in the school up to and including the seniors about my horseback riding adventure. The nicer people grinned at me, and the others laughed and made comments. I simply did not look up. Toward the end of the week they began to lose interest.

Today in English class Oliver had to give an oral report, and he did it on ospreys. I thought it was very interesting, although everyone else seemed bored. He is shy in front of the class, and I will have to admit he is no orator. But the subject matter was very interesting. He told how DDT has gotten into the ospreys' system from eating fish that live in polluted water and it ruins the eggs—makes the shells too thin to work—so the osprey is in danger of dying out. I've seen ospreys, and I like them very much. I don't want them to die out.

After a person gives an oral report, he has to answer questions, and I tried to think of some intelligent ones. Most of them either asked stupid questions or baited him.

D said, "Who cares about a stupid osprey?"

And the teacher gave her a sharp lecture on conservation that took up so much of the time, I never got to ask any intelligent questions.

When Oliver sat down, the teacher praised him, and Patrick said, "My father says preservationists are some kind of nut."

I said, "Your father is some kind of nut," although I have never spoken to his father. His father is the under-sheriff, and he looks just like Patrick, so he must be some kind of nut.

The teacher said to me, "Let's try to keep the discussion on a higher level that that."

But how can you be high level with ignorant people?

Which reminded me to stop by the newspaper office and thank the editor for printing my letter. It came out in last night's paper, just the way I'd written it. I watched Katherine like a hawk to see if she'd comment on the fine style or anything, but I don't think she even read it.

When I got to the newspaper office, Patrick's father was there, by an odd coincidence. He was talking to Mr. Faber, the editor, a very nice man with a bald head. Patrick's father was speaking rather loudly, which I think is his normal tone of voice.

"That half-assed letter in your paper last night about Northwest Lumber," he was saying. "Where do you come off at printing that kind of garbage?"

"It's the voice of the people, Charlie," Mr. Faber said, and he gave me a kind of flick of his eyes that said "listen but say nothing." Patrick's father didn't even notice me. I doubt if he notices children, except possibly his own.

"It's Communist garbage."

"What do you want me to do about it? Call J. Edgar Hoover?"

Mr. Faber is not a very big man, but he's brave.

"Just don't print any more of that stuff. I had a complaint from Jennings, out at Northwest."

"Oh, that's right. You work for them, off and on, don't you?"

"Goddam right I do."

"So naturally you want to protect your own vested interests."

Patrick's father glowered. "Don't give me none of that college-boy lip," he said.

"Sorry, Charlie," Mr. Faber said. "I forgot your limitations."

I thought Patrick's father was going to hit him. I looked around for a weapon to hand to Mr. Faber, but all I could find was a stapler. I picked it up.

"I represent the law, Faber," Patrick's father said. "I can give you a hell of a lot of trouble."

"Charlie, trouble is my daily fare." Mr. Faber turned his back on Patrick's father and sat down at his typewriter. Then he looked up as if he was surprised to find him still there. "Thanks for dropping in, Charlie. It's good to know you care."

"If I find that Unum bum," Patrick's father said, "I'll lock him up."

75

"On what grounds? Pernicious truth-telling?"

"Never mind grounds. I can always find grounds."

"I'm sure of that. Well, look him up in the phone book. Under U."

"I'll do that." He nearly bumped into me on the way out. He looked down at the stapler in my hand, kind of puzzled for a second and then he put me out of his mind (if any) and went on out.

"It's good to know that law and order still prevail," Mr. Faber said. "How are you, Marianne?"

"Fine. Thank you for printing my letter."

He sighed. "You're welcome."

"I hope it won't cause you any trouble."

"Well, as I just told Charlie—"

He looked as if he had a lot to do, so I said thanks again and started out. Then I remembered the stapler, and I brought it back. He laughed. "Were you going to protect me?"

"Yes."

"Good girl."

I went home and wrote another letter to the paper:

To the Editor:

May I commend you on your forthrightness and courage in printing the splendid letter from E Pluribus Unum recommending action against the Northwest Lumber Company. Editorial honesty such as yours, sir, in the face of whatever threats from the ignorant and uninformed, cheer those of us who would protect this splendid land from the ravages of the enemy.

Signed:

Direct Descendant of Tom Paine

76

THIRTEEN

TONIGHT when Dr. Goodwin, Dr. Francis, and Mr. Bartlett came for their evening of bridge, Dr. Francis brought Katherine a new record album. She looked at it and lit up like a Christmas tree. "Joan Sutherland! Oh, Francis, how nice." She put it on the record player and although they dealt their hands at the card table, mostly they sat and listened to the record.

Personally I don't like opera singers. I saw *Aïda* once and to this day I don't know what all those people were supposed to be doing. So I sort of casually put my hands over my ears and curled up in my chair in the corner with *The Heart of Darkness,* which I'm struggling with for English.

The phone rang, the way it always does when Dr. Francis is here, and he had to tell some woman to give her child two baby aspirin and call him back if it didn't seem any better.

I kind of fell asleep, and when I woke up, Katherine

was taking the record off and saying, "She *is* marvelous, isn't she." And Dr. Goodwin said kind of dreamily, "The last time Matilda and I were in London, we went to the opera . . ." And Mr. Bartlett, who I never would take to be an opera man, was smiling happily. Well, to each his own, I always say.

They played some bridge, and at eleven I helped Katherine bring in the quiche Lorraine and the coffee. She said to the others, "To go from the sublime to the ridiculous, under-sheriff Bell asked me for a job today."

"What kind of job?" Dr. Francis said.

"He wants Oliver's job. He says he can do twice the work. Oliver, he says, is a no-good, lazy Indian."

I was really paying attention now.

"Charlie was never one to crucify himself for the human race," Dr. Goodwin said.

And I said, "What did you tell him?"

She smiled. "I told him I was quite satisfied with Oliver."

"And then what?" Dr. Francis said. "Charlie can get mean."

Katherine poured black coffee into one of the Spode cups and handed it to Mr. Bartlett. "Well, he tried. He was rather insulting, in fact, and I had to run him off the place."

Mr. Bartlett said, "How did you do that, Kit?"

"I told him to get off my property, and I raised my sturdy cane. That cane is very useful, you know."

Mr. Bartlett said, "Don't tangle with Charlie Bell, Kit. He's got a mean temper."

"Somewhere in the depths of his cloudy mind, he recognizes his inferiority and it makes him mad," Dr.

78

Goodwin said.

"Oh, I'm not afraid of Charlie Bell. He reminds me of one of Faulkner's Snopeses."

The quiche Lorraine was marvelous. I moved in for a second piece.

Somebody said something about Charlie Bell's son, and I pricked up my ears.

"Chip off the old block," Mr. Bartlett said.

"He's a mean, nasty monster," I said, and they laughed. Adults laugh at the strangest things.

"Well, he's never had a mother," Katherine said. "One has to make allowances."

I said, "Everybody has a mother."

"His ran away with a fiddle player when he was a baby," Dr. Goodwin said. "Charlie was fit to be tied. He kind of went downhill after that."

I didn't want to have to feel sorry for Patrick Bell. "He could pull himself together and act human."

Dr. Francis said something about youth and rebellion, and a campus riot back East. That was a mistake. Katherine hates to hear about unpleasant current events. She made him stop. Later when they were going home, he said, "I'm sorry I brought up that unpleasant stuff. One sees it on the TV and it sticks in the mind. It's so hard to tell, just looking at it like that, who's in the right."

"Violence is always wrong," Katherine said.

"I guess you're right. . . ." He gave her a quick smile, and he has a very nice smile. "But I'm not absolutely sure." He patted her on the shoulder. "It was a nice evening. It always is."

When they were gone, she said, "Let's listen to that last side one more time."

I tried to keep awake while Miss Sutherland did her stuff. Actually, she does have a pretty fabulous voice. Personally, I can't carry a tune from *do* to *re*.

When it was over, Katherine had her head leaning against the wall and her eyes closed. "Those are the things I like to think about," she said. "Keep a list of beautiful things, and they'll sustain you all your life."

I was interested to know that she made lists, too. "What do you have on your list?"

She smiled without opening her eyes. "It's a long one. Artur Rubinstein, Martha Graham, Cornell's *Juliet,* the Sistine Chapel . . ." She paused. "Hampstead Heath in the spring. Santa Fe at Christmas. Our wedding. Oh, there are so many." She kept her eyes closed so long, I wondered if I should go upstairs. Then she said, "And my husband reciting *Dover Beach* to me. He had a beautiful voice." She said the lines slowly:

"Ah, love, let us be true
To one another! For the world, which seems
To lie before us like a land of dreams,
So various, so beautiful, so new,
Hath really neither joy, nor love, nor light,
Nor certitude, nor peace, nor help for pain;
And we are here as on a darkling plain
Swept with confused alarms of struggle and flight,
Where ignorant armies clash by night."

It was nice, the way she said the lines. Since she still sat there with her eyes closed, I said, "You must have been a good actress."

She opened her eyes and looked at me, as my mother

80

would have said, "with the look that once thrilled thousands." "You think I'm a fraud, don't you. An old lady sitting out here in the country pretending she was once a great star." She laughed, a funny kind of little laugh. "Well, you may be right. I might already have done my best work. And then again . . ." she shrugged and got up. "But I was in love, and I don't regret a minute of my later life. Now, you'd better get to bed. It's disgracefully late."

I went. I can still hear her downstairs. First she puttered around in the kitchen and now she's playing records again with the volume down low. She's certainly an unusual kind of grandmother for a person to have.

FOURTEEN

YESTERDAY WAS FRIDAY, a day of infamy.

D was furious because she couldn't answer a question about Macaulay's essay on Samuel Johnson, and I could. The teacher said, "Why don't you do your homework the way Marianne does? Why don't you use your head? You ought to be ashamed."

I guess she meant well, but that's not the way to achieve instant popularity for a student. Oliver had cut class to go to the university for a placement test, so I couldn't even look at him for moral support. Not that he would have paid any attention to me—he never does in school.

During lunch I went out on the swing and was eating my sandwich when A, B, C and D came storming up to me.

"Who do you think you are?" D said.

I took the slice of olive out of my sandwich and ate it,

not even looking at them. Then D grabbed me by the back of my hair. It hurt.

"I'm Marianne Temple," I said, "and get off my hair." She was twisting it, and it really hurt.

"Cool it," B said to her. "Mrs. Anderson is over there."

Mrs. Anderson is the second grade teacher. D let go of my hair. "Tell me," she said, trying to sound insulting and succeeding quite well. "What are you doing here anyway? Where are your parents?"

"In Europe," I said, "not that it's any of your business."

"That's what you say," C said. C isn't too bright. She's given to clichés.

"Why should I prevaricate?" I said.

C sniffed. "Whatever that means." She is really quite ignorant.

"I think her parents have abandoned her," D said. "That's what I think."

"Oh, don't be asinine," I said.

"I think," D said, "that they're off getting divorced or something, and they don't want to be bothered with this brat kid so they dumped her out here."

I had the feeling that I might suffocate. I could feel the ropes of the swing hurting my hands, I was holding them so tight.

"I bet her grandmother doesn't want her out here," B said.

"She does, too," I said. My chest was hurting.

"Naturally not," D said. "The great actress. . . . I mean having this kid around must interfere with her life style."

"Oh, knock it off," A said. "Leave the dope alone."

83

"The great actress," D said, ignoring A. "My mother says she never heard of her. My mother says she probably never was on a real stage in her whole life."

"She played with the Lunts," I said.

"Whoever they are," C said.

I would have given anything to have had my gunbelt.

"What does she do with you when her boyfriends come to call?" D said.

C giggled. "Does that old woman have boyfriends?"

"Haven't you heard?" D said. "She's got a regular orgy going there every Saturday night. She and old man Bartlett and Doc Goodwin and that young queer, the new doctor, they all get drunk, and then. . . . wellll!" She rolled her eyes. "Who knows?"

"You stupid jerk," I said. I got up.

"Listen, my mother knows about that woman. Everybody in town knows. Don't pull any airs with me. Your grandmother is nothing but an old . . ." She never got to finish her sentence because I punched her in the stomach.

She screamed and fell over backward. Suddenly we were surrounded by kids and Mrs. Anderson. I heard Patrick saying, "I saw it all, Mrs. Anderson, She hit that girl, right in the gut."

D was howling, and C kept saying, "She has chronic appendicitis. This may be the end of her."

It was just my luck to hit a kid with chronic appendicitis. And in the stomach.

A couple of other teachers were there by this time, and Mrs. Anderson was hauling us off to the principal's office. They asked me a lot of questions but I took the Fifth Amendment. I was suspended from school for two days.

*　*　*

When I got home, Katherine was in the kitchen getting ready to cook the ducks that Francis had brought her. They were four blue-winged teal, and I had seen them with their lovely purple heads still on their necks and the little white half-circle that goes across their eyes and the blue shoulders. Now they lay on the chopping block, headless, featherless, and Katherine stood over them with a cleaver.

For a minute she didn't even look up. Somebody had to say something . . . nature abhors a vacuum . . . so I said, "Hello."

Then she did look up and I wished she hadn't. "The school called me."

"Oh. I thought they might."

She waited, I guess for me to explain, but I couldn't think of anything to say. "Did you hit that child?"

"Yes."

"Why?"

Well, I couldn't say "Because she practically called you a whore," so I said nothing.

"They say the child isn't well—chronic appendicitis or something. The parents may sue me." Katherine was really upset. She walked up and down the kitchen. "I know young people today are not strong on self control, but I thought my granddaughter would have some sense of . . . some sense of grace." She stopped by the window and stared out. When she spoke again, she sounded tired. "I'm too old for this kind of thing. Cassandra shouldn't have asked it of me."

I went upstairs. There was a postcard from my mother on the bureau, postmarked Mexico City, and a letter

85

from my father, postmarked London. The card said, "Mexico is terribly gay and colorful. Went to the gardens at Xochimilco today. They are lovely. Thought of you. Love, Mother."

I turned the card over and looked at all these flowers floating in the water. Out loud I said, "Thanks a lot. Thanks a lot for thinking of me."

Before I read my father's letter, I took a shower and put on my pajamas and my gunbelt. "Dear Tippy:" it said. He has handwriting like a bird's tracks in the mud. "I want you to know that I love you and I did my very best—I swear it. Sometimes things are just beyond our control. Believe me, I am thinking of you. Your mother will explain it all. I cannot. I love you—Dad."

After a while, maybe twenty-five years or so, Katherine knocked on the door. "Dinner is ready," she said.

"I don't think I can eat any dinner," I said. "I have a headache."

There was a pause. Then she said, "Can I get you anything?"

"No, thank you. I'll be okay."

I heard the cane on the stairs. I could smell the ducks cooking. I was really very hungry, and the ducks would be no doubt delicious. Kill, kill; devour, devour.

I finally fell asleep and dreamed that I was drowning in a lake full of blossoms. I woke up choking and found I'd crammed the corner of my pillow into my mouth.

It was dark and I didn't turn the light on to find out what time it was. It didn't really make any difference. I thought about the blind buck and his doe, the osprey with the broken wing, and how hard everybody tries to keep going no matter what disaster befalls them. Even when nobody wants you, you keep on going, and it seems stupid but there you are. I couldn't think of any way of committing suicide that would not either hurt or be so messy that everybody would hate me for having to clean up after me.

I fell asleep again and this time when I woke up, there was that funny kind of lightness inside the dark that tells you it's going to be dawn in a few minutes. I got up and dressed, silently. Although I hadn't thought about it consciously, I knew what I was going to do. I was going to go to Oliver's house and ask him to see about getting me into the reservation. I could learn to chew hides into leather and things like that. In spite of my braces, my teeth are solid.

I packed a few essentials in my smallest suitcase and took my tape recorder. I let myself out of the house as silent as a ghost. Walking down the little dirt road that goes to Oliver's house was scary. There were shadows in all the bushes, and things seemed to be lurking behind the trees. I jumped almost out of my squaw boots when I heard a terribly eerie cry, and I started to run. I tripped over a root in the road and almost fell down. I heard the cry again, I thought I was going to faint. Then all of a sudden I realized it was an owl. Dougie, who is full of animal stories, told me an owl means death, but I don't believe that kind of silly superstition.

I walked fast down the road. Once I thought I saw a snake, but it turned out to be a dead branch. My heart was banging against my ribs like a drum.

Just when I thought I couldn't stand it any longer to be out there in the wilderness alone, I saw Oliver's house. I'd seen it before, but I'd never been inside. It's a little wooden house with no paint on it and some of the shingles are missing. The glass in the one window on the side facing the street is cracked. Oliver said it's about a hundred years old, and Mrs. Foxtail bought it for fifty dollars. Some hens were pecking around in the dirt in front of the house.

There was a light shining inside, and as far as I was concerned right then, it was the most beautiful house in the whole world. I ran up to the rickety door and knocked. Dougie opened it. He didn't look surprised to see me. One of the nicer things about Indians is that they don't act astonished all the time. "Hi," he said, and he opened the door wide for me to come in.

Mrs. Foxtail was cooking on a stove that was a big oil drum. She was frying eggs, and I could smell coffee. I was suddenly so hungry I thought I'd collapse.

She gave me her broad smile that makes all her wrinkles arrange themselves in little patterns. "Come in, come in. Sit down, sit down."

I sat down on a nail keg. The walls of the room were covered with cardboard, turned dark gray by smoke. There was a sink with a faucet, a couple of wooden chairs, a mattress on the floor in the corner, and a table with two broken legs that were propped up by a tomato juice can and an overturned bucket. On one wall there was a calendar with a picture of Flathead Lake.

Beyond this room I could see the bedroom, with a couple of cots. Oliver came out of the bedroom, putting on his sweater. He didn't look surprised either. "Hi."

"Hi." I tried to think how to explain why I was there. "I hope you don't mind my dropping in. I was just passing by . . ." No, this was no time for the social amenities. "I wanted to talk to you," I said. "I want . . ."

He held up his hand. "Have breakfast first. Never talk on an empty stomach." He gave me a nice grin. He has pretty white teeth, and I'm glad he doesn't have to wear braces.

Dougie helped Mrs. Foxtail put the food on the table. There was fried bread, too. I ate like a condemned prisoner at his last meal.

Mrs. Foxtail kept loading up my plate, and nobody talked except to say, "More coffee, please," or something like that.

Then we were through, and Oliver was right—I did feel better.

"I want to go live on a reservation," I said.

He raised that one crazy eyebrow. "Why?"

"Personal reason."

"Let's go for a walk," he said.

I offered to help Mrs. Foxtail with the dishes, but she said no and beamed at me. Dougie went out to feed the chickens.

Oliver and I walked across a field to a little lake. I hadn't been there before. It was a green lake. I wanted to ask him what made it green but there were more important things to discuss. We sat down on a log.

"My grandmother doesn't want me and apparently my parents are . . ." I took a deep breath. ". . . having a little trouble. I don't think they can cope with me right now. I have to go somewhere, and I think I'd be happy on a reservation."

Oliver chewed on a pine needle and stared into the green water. Finally, he said, "I don't think life on a reservation is quite what you think it is. For one thing,

Indians are very poor. You saw how we live, and we're better off than a lot of them."

"What they need is to unite," I said. I'd been thinking about this for some time. "Red power is what you Indians need."

He smiled. "You've been reading the papers. Well, it may be true. Me, I don't like power—white or red or black or whatever. People use power to grind down other people. I just don't like it."

"But you're wrong. Solidarity, brotherhood, that's what you need. I could help them work for that. I'm a good organizer."

"The Indian tribes have no feeling of unity among themselves," he said. "What you don't see is that a Navajo for instance is just as different from a Blackfeet as an Irishman is different from a Jew."

"You're just copping out," I said. "You're just being an Uncle Tomahawk."

He laughed. "Where did you read that?"

"But you are."

"I just like to be in the woods. I trust animals a lot more than I trust man, any kind of man."

"I want to work for the betterment of the Indian."

"Marianne, you're a good kid. But you don't know anything about Indians. And Indians aren't too happy about having white people barge in and tell them how to run their lives. That's what's been wrong all along."

I said, "Oh, you're so superior. I am going to live on the reservation. Period."

"Nobody would let you. The Indians wouldn't, your family wouldn't, the government wouldn't. . . . Face facts, kid. Stop romanticizing everything. It does too much damage." He flipped a flat stone into the water and it skipped four times. I've tried and tried to do that. "And you've got to think of things from your grandmother's point of view. It's not easy at her age to take on a teen-ager. She's gotten set in her ways, and whammo! here you come. Give her a chance to get used to you. It doesn't mean she doesn't like you."

Neither of us said anything for a long time. What could I say? He was so darned stubborn. I watched a duck lift up off the other end of the lake and fly away with that long graceful neck sticking out in front, and I thought of the blue-winged teals.

"Well, I might as well go home," I said, "for all the help you are."

He looked at his Timex watch. "Your grandmother will be out riding. You can get back in the house and she'll never know you were gone."

We stopped to pick up my suitcase, and I let Dougie talk on the tape recorder. His voice is small, and I didn't have the volume high enough so it didn't record, but more or less what he said was:

"I am Dougie Three-Toes. I am a Kootenai. I am seven years old. I live with my aunt and my brother Oliver. I feed the chickens. I love my rooster. When I grow up, I am going to be a truck driver."

When Oliver left me at the house, before he went out to the barn to do the chores, he said, "If you want, I'll take you to see my osprey tomorrow."

FIFTEEN

I'D NEVER REALLY PAID any attention to scenery; in fact, I found the subject boring. The only thing I could ever get stirred up about was the Charles River at night, from the Cambridge side, when it looks like black velvet with a bunch of diamonds tossed across it. And on the other side, Boston in the dark looks like one big enchanted castle with a moat. I liked to think of Paul Revere rowing across the river with his oars muffled. That was good thinking. Paul Revere is one of my heroes, and I don't care if he did get captured outside of Lexington—he talked his way out of it. He used his brains.

So Oliver and Dougie took me out to see the osprey. We went through the woods a way I hadn't been before, past the trail that goes to the ranger's cabin, and we came to a pretty big lake with an island in it. The osprey was on the island. You have to get out there in a boat that

Oliver keeps hidden in the bushes. It's a beat-up old row-boat, and I never thought I'd live to see that osprey. The wind was blowing the water around, and the boat leaked. Dougie bailed water with an old tin can, and the waves banged the boat and cold water kept hitting me in the face and sloshing up around my ankles. I was blue.

"You can swim, can't you?" Oliver said.

"Of course." I can, actually. If the circumstances are desperate enough, I can swim for a few minutes, except that I would probably be immobilized by fear. Did I mention that I nearly drowned at that awful camp, when some wise guy junior counselor pushed me off the end of the dock? She was allegedly trying to get me used to deep water. What she did was to give me psychic scars that I'll carry to the grave.

But finally we landed on a little gravel beach on the island, and as soon as I got out of that boat, I began to enjoy it. All you could see anywhere was lake and sky and woods, and it was tremendous. Right after I got out of the boat, Oliver pointed to the sky, and there was a huge straggly wedge of great big beautiful birds flying south. He said they were Canada geese. We watched them till they were out of sight. You could hear them honking, two notes like an old-fashioned automobile horn.

We walked about halfway around the island, part of the way on the little strip of beach, and in places where the trees came right down to the water, on a narrow path that was so faint it was hard to see, although Oliver and Dougie had no problem following it. But of course, they go out there all the time to feed the osprey

Dougie was wearing a crazy hat that he wears a lot.

I guess it was once a cowboy hat, but it's so old and it's gotten wet and knocked around so much, it has no shape at all. It's kind of like Hoss Cartright's. It's a little too big for him, and it makes him look like a smiling mushroom. Anyway he took off his hat and filled it with chokecherries. I really wanted to wash mine off, but I didn't want to hurt Dougie's feelings so I ate them straight from the hat. It's not that Dougie isn't clean—Mrs. Foxtail and both the boys are very, very clean—but who knows where that hat has been. Well, it didn't kill me. The chokecherries were good, but they pucker your mouth. Dougie showed me how to pop the juice in my mouth and spit out the seeds. That would go over big in Boston.

Oliver said there were deer on the island, but we didn't see any.

We came to a big dead tree, and Oliver said, "Hey, Osprey. We're here."

Probably no one will believe me, but this enormous bird hopped down out of the tree and he came right up to Oliver as if he were a pet canary or something. He made a kind of shriek-shriek sound, and Oliver took off the little pack that he carries on his shoulders and pulled out three big trout.

"Dougie caught these for you this morning, Osprey," he said. He tossed the first one to the bird, and the bird tore into it as if he was really hungry, although Oliver feeds him every day or two.

That osprey was fabulous. Oliver said his wingspread is six and a half feet. I'd seen them flying up high, with long narrow wings that are kind of bent, but I'd no idea the bird would be so big close up. It would have been scary if he hadn't been so tame. He wouldn't let me get very close to him, but the boys could go right up to him and touch him. He had a white crown and a black patch over one eye and some dark bands on his tail. He kind of dragged one wing, and Oliver said someone had shot him.

"He's getting better," Dougie said, "but he can't go high yet."

Oliver examined the wing while the bird was eating his second fish. "He's mending all right. Pretty soon he can make it on his own." The silly osprey looked at Oliver and peeped like a chicken. I think he really *liked* him. Imagine walking along Boylston Street with an osprey on a leash.

"How old is he?" I said.

"He's getting along. Probably about twenty years old."

I could hardly believe it. He was six years older than I was. "Doesn't he have a wife or anything?"

"He did, but the eggs didn't hatch. That's what I was talking about in English class; the DDT makes the shells too thin."

I felt terrible about the poor little ospreys that didn't hatch. I sat on the sandy beach watching the osprey and dreaming about how I could live out there and become a well-known person in conservation, possibly even an international authority.

The island would be a good place to live if things ever get too much. As they well might. If I weren't so scared of water; that's the only drawback. But you could probably live out there on fish and berries and stuff like that. Though maybe I'd get poisoned by DDT the way the osprey did. DDT is supposed to be out, but people still use it.

It was getting cold and I was hungry, so I was glad

when Oliver said, "Let's go."

We were back on Standard Time, and the day was ending faster than you'd expect. The sunset over the lake was so pretty I almost forgot to be scared in the boat.

When I got home, Katherine was waiting dinner for me.

"Goodness, where have you been?" she said. I was pretty wet and dirty.

"Out to an island with Oliver and Dougie."

"Oh." If I was with Oliver, it was A-OK with her. She does dote on that boy. "Well, have a hot shower. I'll hold back the dinner."

For Katherine to hold back the dinner without visible signs of annoyance was unusual. I figured she was saying "let bygones be bygones."

The gentlemen callers came that night instead of their usual Saturday, because they'd all gone to a basketball game the night before. They'd invited me, but I said I had to study. I am not sports-minded, and all a school gym does is to remind me of my own athletic shortcomings.

I was pretty sleepy after the afternoon on the island and all, and I kept falling asleep in my chair. Katherine asked me if I shouldn't go to bed, but I was afraid I'd miss something interesting—like food—so I said no.

I came awake in a hurry when I heard Dr. Francis mention the letters I had sent to the paper, though of course they didn't know I had sent them. They were laughing about them. Humor was far from my intention.

"The style is marvelous," Dr. Francis said. Only he didn't really mean marvelous. "I think somebody is putting us on."

"Well, it might do some good just the same," Dr. Goodwin said. "It doesn't hurt to call attention to those things. Northwest has been clear-cutting and polluting for years."

When Katherine brought in the fondue and the coffee, Dr. Francis cleared his throat and took off his dark-rimmed glasses and put them back on again. "Katherine . . ."

She looked at him as if she was fond of him, which she is. "What is it, Francis?"

"Well . . ." He looked at the other men, and Dr. Goodwin nodded as if he was encouraging him. "I've been delegated to ask you . . ." The phone rang right then, and he looked relieved. "It's probably for me." He jumped up to answer it in the study.

We could hear him talking. "Yes, Mrs. Jeffrey," he said. "Give him a nitroglycerin and have him breathe into a paper bag."

I couldn't believe it. "Nitroglycerin! Breathe into a paper bag? What is he *doing?*" I know Mrs. Jeffrey's son. He is a freshman and he has something wrong with his heart.

"Call me back in fifteen minutes," Dr. Francis said.

Dr. Goodwin looked at me and smiled. "The nitro is for his heart. The paper bag is to get him to rebreathe the carbon dioxide he's losing too fast. Francis isn't trying to kill him."

I still say you'd think the medical profession could come up with something more scientific than a paper bag.

When Dr. Francis came back, Katherine said, "What

97

were you going to ask me?"

"Oh, yes," he said, as if he'd almost forgotten. "Well, the church wants to do an evening of drama, and the committee wanted me to ask you if you'd do some scenes from *Antigone*."

Katherine looked almost shocked. "Do some scenes? Francis, it's been so many years."

I happen to have read *Antigone* last year for speech class. "That's ridiculous," I said. "Antigone is a young girl."

I guess it wasn't my most tactful statement, and I was sorry I'd said it. Katherine looked hurt for just a second, and then she laughed. Dr. Francis looked furious.

"Marianne is right," she said. "Antigone is a teen-ager."

"What of it?" Dr. Francis said. "You said yourself that Cornell at thirty-five was a magnificent Juliet."

"And Bernhardt played *L'Aiglon* when she was fifty-six," Dr. Goodwin said.

"Lord, Joe, how do you know that?" Mr. Bartlett said.

"I looked it up because I knew Katherine would say she was too old."

Katherine was looking thoughtful, as if she really wanted to do it, and I was appalled. I could just see her getting up there and making a complete fool of herself. The four witches and their gossipy mothers and all those other awful people would scream with joy. "Katherine is *sixty-five*," I said.

"Oh, be quiet, Marianne," Dr. Francis said. He had never spoken sharply to me before, and I was both scared and mad.

"And who would play Creon?" Katherine said.

"Francis will," Dr. Goodwin said. "After all, he's always bragging about the plays he was in, in college."

By this time I should have left the room, but I couldn't just let this happen. "Creon is Antigone's *uncle*," I said.

Mr. Bartlett refilled his coffee cup. He is always very nice to me, so he just said, very nicely, "I think they can bring it off, Marianne."

Well, nobody is going to listen to me, that's for sure. I think my attitude even partly prompted Katherine to consider it, like a dare or something. "I'll think about it," she said, and she had a little gleam in her eye that I hadn't ever seen before.

I went up to bed without finishing my fondue. The phone is ringing. I suppose it's about the Jeffrey boy and his paper bag.

SIXTEEN

TODAY AT SCHOOL Patrick was trying to impress
D. D has a thing for Oliver. Half the time she insults
him, and half the time she wheedles around him and
acts like the flirt in a 1930's movie. Oliver just walks
away, and it makes her furious. This afternoon Patrick
was laughing at her because she—quote—couldn't even
make it with a lousy Indian. Oliver left. Sometimes I
wish he'd punch Patrick right in the nose. I'll bet Sitting
Bull would have.

Then Patrick started in on me. He calls me "Tin-
Tooth" when he wants to be particularly offensive. He
kept saying, "How about a date, Tin-Tooth? Let's you
and me have a hot date tonight, whaddaya say?" Appre-
ciative laughter from the audience. D and her friends
sort of steer clear of me since I punched her, and that is
fine with me. So they just stood around giggling. Patrick
made a grab for me, and I kicked him in the shin. Boots

are good for kicking shins. He didn't think it was funny, but everybody else laughed. People will laugh at their own best friends if they get hurt. Ignorance and cruelty at every turn.

When I got home, Oliver and Katherine were currying the horses and having a conversation. I sat down on a sack of grain and listened. Oliver was saying that he thought sometimes he ought to get a degree in law or medicine so he could help his people.

"If you don't want to be a lawyer or a doctor," Katherine said, "it doesn't make sense to be one. Do you want to be one?"

"No."

"All right then. If you are an effective person in your own field, that will do your people as much good as anything. I really believe, Oliver, that what the Indians need most is to feel pride in themselves."

"Well, I don't know," he said, but I could tell he wanted to be convinced. "Maybe going into wildlife management is just a way of copping out."

"Don't use those stupid clichés," Katherine said. "And of course it isn't. What can be more important than environment? It's something everybody says nowadays, but how many get right down and work for it? Good people are needed in that area, and I don't know anyone who could do a better job than you."

The grain made me sneeze.

"Hello, Marianne," she said.

"Hello." I wish she would have serious conversations with me sometimes, but she never does. We just observe the amenities. She thinks I'm a child.

Dougie showed up from nowhere and squatted down

beside me on the floor. He had a purple flower tucked over his ear. I have never felt any particular fondness for young children, but I really like Dougie.

"You've got a tick on your arm," he said.

"What?" I thought I misunderstood him, but he poked the inside of my arm, just below the elbow. There was this horrible bug hanging onto me for dear life. I tried to brush it off, but it stuck. The thing wriggled. I screamed.

"Good God," Katherine said. "What happened?"

"Tick," Dougie said.

I closed my eyes and screamed again.

"Stop that racket." Katherine took hold of my arm and poked at the awful thing. She tried to pull it off, and it wouldn't come.

"Be careful," Oliver said. "Don't leave the head in."

I've heard of Rocky Mountain Spotted Fever; I knew my end had come. I was too frightened to faint.

"Have you got a match?" Oliver said.

Katherine fished a pack of matches out of her pocket and struck one. She was coming at me with this lighted flame. I tried to pull away, but she held my arm in a vice-like grip. "Sit still, Marianne. Nobody's going to hurt you." And right before my very eyes she held the match to my arm. Well, not *right* on my arm but up against the bug. It curled up and dropped off. I thought I'd die.

"Don't make such a fuss," Katherine said. "It's just a tick. Put a little iodine on your arm." And she went back to currying her horse as if nothing at all had threatened my very life.

Dougie followed me into the house and watched while I poured practically a bottle of iodine all over my arm. Then I went into the bathroom and threw up.

When I came out, Dougie was still there. "I don't think you'll die," he said. "I get ticks all the time."

"You probably have an immunity," I said. "I don't."

"I don't have nothin'; not even that stuff." He pointed to the iodine. Then Oliver whistled for him. "I hope you don't die, Marianne," he said as he left. "I like you."

So far, I haven't died.

SEVENTEEN

TODAY there were two letters to the editor and a news story connected with my letters. The first letter said I was a Communist rabble-rouser and a threat to free enterprise, and the other one said I was a voice crying in the wilderness that should be listened to by all those who cared about the future of their country. The news story said that a group of women "encouraged by the current comments in the Letters-to-the-Editor column of our local paper concerning environment," had set up a committee to combat pollution in all its forms. They invited the women of the community to join. They are calling themselves GOLPS, Girls Opposed to Local Pollution. They said they hoped to meet with the writers of the letters. I hope Mr. Faber doesn't give me away.

When Dr. Francis came over after dinner to rehearse *Antigone* which, by the way, Katherine has agreed to do, he said, "Katherine, are you going to join GOLPS?"

She snorted. "Thank you. I'm not a joiner."

"It's a good cause," he said.

"You don't want Montana to smell like New York, do you?" I said.

"I've forgotten how New York smells."

"Like something that's been dead a long time."

"A lot worse than when you lived there, Katherine," Dr. Francis said. He's been to New York three times. But I guess that's enough to know how it smells.

"I detest groups of women," Katherine said.

He laughed. "You're a lone wolf."

They got out their copies of *Antigone* and I went out to the barn. It makes me very nervous to hear them read their lines. I am so afraid Katherine will be a laughing stock—and in front of all those people, like D's mother. I will be publicly humiliated.

I have taken to sitting in the barn a good deal. I like it. There's just enough light to read in the day, if you don't mind straining your eyes a little. And at night I can always use a flashlight. It's quiet and private and it smells nice and barny. The weather has been really warm most of the time, and the barn has a nice coolness. The horses stomp their feet and chew on their hay and sometimes look over their shoulders to see what I'm doing. I really like them as long as I don't have to get on them. Horses just sort of take you for granted if you leave them alone, and I think that's the best way to treat people.

Sometimes Oliver comes back in the evening to finish up his chores, sweeping out the barn and watering the horses and all that. Tonight he didn't come till late.

I got tired of reading, finally, so I wandered around and looked at the old pictures on the walls, most of them of horses that Ben Carter had. There's an enlarged snapshot of the ranch house they used to have. It looks really neat-o. I wish I could see it, but Katherine sold it a long time ago and she doesn't seem to want to go out there again. I guess it makes her sad. Or maybe she hated it—I don't know.

I heard Dr. Francis drive off, and I was just going in the house when Oliver showed up. He looked gloomy, and he didn't have much to say.

"What's the matter with you?" I said.

"I'm mad."

"Who at?"

"Somebody dumped a dead skunk in front of our door. It'll stink for a week."

"Who would do a rotten thing like that?"

He raised that eyebrow. "Dougie saw a blue dune-buggy driving off."

"Oh, no!"

"Oh, yes."

Patrick has a blue dune-buggy. Not too many people do.

"You'd better tell the sheriff."

"You forgot something. The sheriff is his father." He pitched down some hay, and Candida whinnied.

"Well, tell the real sheriff."

"He's in Great Falls, riding in a rodeo with his posse. He's always off somewhere riding with that stupid posse. Anyway, he wouldn't believe me. Not my word against Patrick's."

"That's unjust. That's disgusting."

"That's life." He filled the water buckets.

I wanted to shake him for giving in so easily. "Where is your courage?" I said. "What would Sitting Bull do in a case like this?"

He laughed. "Hightail it for Canada."

"Oh, you're hopeless."

"I know. Dougie and I are going hunting after school tomorrow. You want to come?"

"What are you going to hunt?"

"Deer."

I was appalled. "You mean you're going to kill deer?"

"*A* deer." He turned off the water and came over to me. "Listen, dum-dum, my family has to eat. I don't like to kill deer—you know how I feel about animals. But we have to eat."

He was upset, so I didn't argue with him any more. I knew he was upset because mean as he is, he never calls me mean names like "dum-dum." "Okay," I said, "I'll go."

After he'd gone, I came up to my room. Katherine is already in bed, reading. I can see the slice of light under her door.

To the Editor:

Sir:

Is justice dead? Has the American Indian no recourse to justice even today? We ravaged his land and decimated his tribes and now we deny him simple everyday consideration. He is a peaceful—nay, even meek—member of our society. Do we abuse him out of sadism? He is a good man and good men are at a premium. Let us remember the words of that great leader, Chief Joseph, and I quote: "From where the sun now stands, I will fight no more forever." Unquote. In very truth, we can do no other.

Signed:
Concerned Paleface.

EIGHTEEN

IT HAS BEEN SAID that I exaggerate. I admit it. But it would be impossible to exaggerate the events that took place today. They speak for themselves.

After school I set out with Oliver and Dougie. To my surprise Oliver was carrying a bow and arrow. He says he doesn't like to shoot an animal, and he is very accurate with a bow and arrow. He told me about ten times that when he shoots a deer, it dies instantly. I can tell he doesn't like to kill them.

Dougie was wearing his crazy old hat, and he had stuck a bright blue mountain jay's feather into it with a safety pin. Both he and Oliver were wearing rucksacks, and they had strips of orange flannel pinned to their shirts. Oliver had one for me. He said it was a law that anyone hunting had to wear orange somewhere. I told him I wasn't hunting anything, but he said, "Don't argue," and he pinned it on my sleeve.

He had a quiver with arrows in it and a really pretty bow that he made himself. It's called a recurve bow and it's made of wood and horn and sinew, just like an old Indian bow, he said.

We walked for a long time through the woods. The afternoon was warm and sunny, and it was nice to be out. My only problem is I'm always stubbing my toe over roots and things, and that was kind of irritating to Oliver because he wanted us to be quiet. I don't know why he invites me if I'm so much trouble.

Once he stopped short, and I almost fell over him. I thought he'd seen a deer but he stooped over and picked up something, a metal thing.

"What is it?" I asked.

"A shell casing." He looked at it, frowning. "The season doesn't open till next week."

"How come we're hunting then?"

"Archers get a special season."

After a while he came to a place I guess he'd been heading for. He stationed Dougie and me in a little bunch of bushes and told us to be still. Dougie clapped his hand over his mouth and giggled silently. That crazy little kid.

"If you get a deer," I said, "how do you get it home?" I could see myself carrying a haunch over my shoulder, like Friar Tuck.

"I'll dress it out and hang it in a tree, and my uncle will help me bring it in in his pickup."

That was news. I didn't know he even had an uncle.

He left us and went across the clearing and climbed up in the lower branches of a big tree.

We sat and sat and sat. Dougie was almost asleep, and

I was very stiff from sitting so still that long. I wanted to move because some twigs were sticking into me, but I was afraid I'd make too much noise. Dougie's head fell against my shoulder, and his hat slipped over his nose. This hat has a tall smooth crown with water stains, and the brim is so battered it curls up on the sides like wood shavings. It's an insane hat, and, to tell the truth, I wish I had one like it.

Dougie moved, and a twig snapped. Without opening his eyes, he said, "Shhh."

A minute later I saw Oliver move a little. He raised his bow and fitted an arrow. I couldn't see or hear a thing, but he's got some kind of Indian radar. A few seconds later I saw antlers and then a deer coming out of the brush. A doe was with him. I saw Oliver put down the bow. He looked at me and pointed at the buck. It was the blind deer.

The doe acted nervous. I guess she got our scent. She kept pushing at the buck with her head, and she herded him right out of the clearing. In a few seconds they were out of sight.

I felt kind of weak. I couldn't tell, to be perfectly honest, whether I wanted Oliver to get a deer or not. I knew his family needed the meat, and also there *is* some kind of funny excitement about a hunt—there's that suspense and wanting your side to win. But on the other hand I couldn't even let myself imagine what it would be like to see a deer fall dead. They are so beautiful. Anyway I was very glad he'd seen in time that it was our buck and doe.

Just as I was thinking that, there was a loud bang. Oliver was down out of that tree before I even had time to think what might have happened. Dougie jumped up, dropped his hat, grabbed it and ran after Oliver. They were out of sight before I even got to my feet, and I was terrified they were going to leave me there alone. I said, "Hey, wait!" but my voice didn't come out very loud.

Usually when Oliver walks through the forest he doesn't even seem to move a pine needle out of place, but this time he'd gone so fast, he'd smashed through some bushes so I tried to follow his trail. I tried to run, but limbs kept snapping back in my face and things tripped me up.

Just as I was getting really panicked, I found them. They were standing still beside a bunch of thick bushes. The buck was there, and he was pawing the ground and acting frightened.

Then I saw the doe. She lay on her side and she was dead. She already had that unreal look that the moose head in Ben Carter's study has.

"Who did that?" I said. I was trying not to cry. That doe was my friend; I understood her.

Oliver didn't answer. He knelt beside her and took out his hunting knife. He and Dougie got the doe onto her back and Oliver plunged his knife in. I don't know whether I screamed out loud or just in my mind. It was the most awful thing I've ever seen. I went off in the bushes and lay down. My head was spinning, and I thought I was going to be sick. I'd never realized. I'd never even thought how it would be. I can't even talk about it now.

I don't know how long it was before Dougie came and got me. I didn't want to go back with him but he said Oliver said I had to. "Don't be scared, Marianne," he said. He took me by the hand. "Everything's okay."

Oliver was washing his hands in a little stream that ran down off the hillside near us. I was afraid to look at the doe, but I couldn't help it. She was covered up with a cheesecloth and propped up on chunks of dead wood. There was blood on the ground, but the doe didn't look so bad now. Her eyes were closed, and she looked almost as if she was asleep and wearing a nightgown. There was a can of black pepper on the ground. I never did find out what that was for.

The buck was milling around, and every minute or so he would bump into a tree. It was heart-breaking. Oliver looked at him in a kind of despairing way. He went over and led him back into the clearing. A white-tail deer isn't terribly big. This one was only about as high as my shoulder, and I'm not very tall. He had a very black nose with two white bands just behind it and his coat was kind of bluish. The buck stamped his feet and snorted through his nose as Oliver brought him into the clearing.

Then his head shot up and his ears twitched as if he were listening. Oliver turned to listen too. He looked at Dougie, and Dougie melted into the brush so fast and so silently you couldn't even tell he'd been there. Oliver grabbed my arm and pulled me down behind a fallen log. Now I could hear what the buck and Oliver had heard. Men's voices and the sound of twigs snapping and brush moving. Oliver's grip on my arm tightened. I tried not to breathe because I was sure they'd hear me. My heart was banging away in my chest so loud it seemed to echo through the woods.

Then two men came into the clearing. First I saw their guns, and then I saw their faces. It was Patrick and his father. The buck whirled away from them and gave a tremendous bound like a spring uncoiling. He crashed head-on into a tree and fell.

Patrick gave a little yip and lifted his gun to his shoulder. Without making a sound Oliver stood up and fitted an arrow to his bow. The arrow whirred through the air, and the deer fell. Patrick's gun roared, and the bullet hit the deer in the haunch, but he was already dead. Oliver had killed him with one swift accurate arrow in the throat. It was a mercy killing.

Patrick and his father swarmed into that clearing as if they were ten people, big and loud. "I got him, Pop," Patrick said. He kicked at the deer's hindquarters with his stupid boot.

"You did not," I said. "Oliver did."

They hadn't even see me, and they looked really surprised when I stood up. Then Patrick guffawed. "Look who's here. Old Tin-Tooth."

His father was looking at the doe. "Here's the other one we shot," he said. He looked at Oliver with an unpleasant grin. "Thanks for dressing her out."

"The buck is mine," Oliver said.

"The hell it is," Patrick said. "I got him clean as a whistle."

Oliver's mouth was tight. "Look at him. He's got an arrow in his throat."

"You shot him after I did."

Oliver took a step toward him. "You can't hardly kill a buck with a haunch shot."

Patrick's father laughed. "You get lost, Injun."

He started dragging the doe through the brush. "I'll be back directly Pat. You start dressing out the buck, hear?"

"Sure." Patrick pushed the buck over on his back. "My God," he said, "the critter's blind." He laughed. "What do you know about that." He pulled his hunting knife out of his belt.

I picked up a rock and threw it at him. It missed.

"Listen, Tin-Tooth," he said, "watch yourself. I might get mad." He raised the knife, ready to plunge it into the buck.

Oliver leaped at him. Oliver can move almost as fast as a deer. Before Patrick even knew what was happening, Oliver grabbed the knife out of his hand and threw it into the bushes. Patrick roared. For a second he looked as if he didn't know whether to go after the knife or after Oliver. Oliver made up his stupid mind for him. He flew at him. Patrick is about twice as big as Oliver, but Oliver is so quick and so well-coordinated, he could handle almost anybody. Patrick kept lunging at him, and Oliver would dance out of the way and then while Patrick was trying to get his balance, Oliver would hit him.

Patrick's nose was bleeding, and one of his eyes began to close. He started bellowing for his father, and he kept trying to get at his gun that he'd put down on the ground. I inched over toward the gun, and I was just about to grab it when this voice behind me roared. "All right. Cut it out." And there was Patrick's father, levelling his gun at Oliver. He edged over to Patrick's gun and picked it up and threw it at him. That seemed to me like a dangerous thing to do, but Patrick managed to catch it.

"You jerk," Patrick's father said to Patrick. "Can't you handle yourself any better that that?"

Patrick was breathing so hard he could hardly talk.

"Listen, Pop, this guy jumped me . . ."

"Shut up. Pick up the doe and get her into the truck. She's out there." He gestured over his shoulder.

Patrick slunk off, wiping his bloody nose on his sleeve. That is a repulsive boy if I ever saw one.

His father kept the gun pointed at Oliver. "All right, Injun, I'm taking you in."

"What for?" Oliver said. His sleeve was torn and his hair flopped down over his forehead, but he looked a lot better than Patrick. I was proud of him.

"For hunting without a license, to start."

"Indians don't have to have a license."

"All right—assault and battery."

"Are you out of your mind?" I said. "That was Oliver's deer. Patrick is a big stupid bully."

Patrick's father looked me over. "If I was you, sister," he said, "I'd shut my big mouth."

"Don't you talk to me like that," I said, "My grandmother will take care of you."

"Oh? Who's your grandmother?"

Oliver was frowning at me, but I was too mad to pay attention. "Katherine Carter, that's who."

He gave a very nasty laugh. "No kiddin'? Now isn't that something. Well, you tell her, does she have any complaints, she can look me up." He prodded Oliver with the end of his gun. "Get movin'."

They went off through the woods. It got very, very still. Not a bird was singing, and the buck lay there so quiet. Then I remembered Dougie. I hadn't seen him since the goon squad showed up. "Dougie?"

He rose up out of the bushes not six feet away from me.

"You saw what happened."

He nodded.

"What are we going to do?"

He started looking around in the bushes. "Gotta find that knife."

"What for?" I had visions of Dougie attacking Patrick and his father with Patrick's hunting knife.

He found it and came back to the buck. He looked at me.

"I got to dress him out or he'll spoil."

"Do you know how?"

"Yeah. I've watched Ollie lots of times."

But he was so little. I had to hold the buck by the head so he wouldn't roll over while Dougie took care of what had to be done. Once I opened my eyes and saw him rubbing blood all over the buck's stomach. "What's that for?" I said, trying to keep cool.

"Keep off the blowflies," he said.

I was kind of ashamed of myself for being so squeamish.

I helped lift the buck up while Dougie put pieces of wood under him to keep him from spoiling. Dougie was a mess. He went over to the stream where Oliver had washed and plunged his arms and head into the water and scrubbed with some of the fine gravel that was along the edge of the stream.

"Now what?" I said.

He got another piece of cheesecloth from his rucksack and tried to tie it around the buck. I helped, but we couldn't do it as neatly as Oliver had.

"We can't just leave him here, can we?" I said. "Patrick will come back for him or animals will get him."

Dougie thought for several minutes. "I'll go get my uncle. You stay here."

The idea of staying there alone scared me right out of my mind, but I was determined that Patrick was not going to get that buck, not after all Oliver had been through.

"Okay," I said, "but hurry. And tell your uncle that Oliver was hauled off by the sheriff."

Dougie shrugged. "Won't do no good."

"Well, run," I said. And he ran. For a minute I could see the top of his hat bobbing along among the trees and then he was gone.

I think it was the longest hour of my life. The sun was getting very low in the sky and I was scared to death that I'd be stuck out there in the dark. It was also possible that Patrick or his father would come back for the buck; but I wasn't afraid of them, and I was not about to let them have it.

Oliver's bow and arrow were there, and although I have never shot an arrow in my whole life, I practiced pulling the string. The trouble was, the arrow kept falling to the ground. The knife was there, too, kind of icky, so I washed it off.

Some flies were settling on the buck where the cheese-cloth didn't cover, so I got some big ferns and wet them and laid them on him. I wasn't sure it was the right thing to do, but I had to keep kind of puttering around so I wouldn't go stark raving mad with fear. There were a million sounds. Anybody who says the forest is silent has never been there. I could hear animals skittering around, and I couldn't tell if they were chipmunks or mountain lions so, of course, I assumed they were mountain lions.

I read in a book in the library last week that under all but the most unusual circumstances a mountain lion won't attack a person. But it didn't say what the unusual circumstances are. It seemed to me a very unusual circumstance for a girl from Boston, Massachusetts, to be sitting in the middle of a forest beside a dead blind buck with a bow and arrow in her hands and night coming on. How unusual can you get? It also said that sometimes when they attack, it's because they mistake you for an animal. So I decided to talk to myself. That ought to clear up my identity.

I couldn't think right off what to talk about so I recited poetry for a while. I have a kind of total recall about some poems, usually the ones I'd rather not remember, like Longfellow that we had to learn in the eighth grade. I recited a chunk of *Evangeline*.

> "This is the forest primeval. The murmuring pines
>   and the hemlocks,
> Bearded with moss, and in garments green, indis-
>   tinct in the twilight,
> Stand like Druids of eld, with voices sad and pro-
>   phetic,
> Stand like harpers hoar, with beards that rest on
>   their bosoms."

What is a harper hoar? I asked the question out loud.
"What is a harper hoar?"
Then I started the one that goes:

> "In the village churchyard she lies,
> Dust is her beautiful eyes.
>   No more she breathes, nor feels, nor stirs. . . ."

I was just getting into *The Midnight Ride of Paul Revere* when I heard a rustle in back of me. I mean a real *loud* rustle. I turned around so fast I dropped the bow. There was a large animal looking at me with yellow eyes. It looked a little bit like a dog, but not really. It was scrawny and mangy looking, and I think it was a coyote but I'll have to look it up later. For some reason, maybe because it looked like a dog, I wasn't frightened, but I didn't want him bothering the buck, so I finished my verse in a very loud voice:

" '. . . scarcely a man is now alive
WHO REMEMBERS THAT FAMOUS DAY
AND YEAR!'

"Scat! Scat! Get out of here!"

And he did. He gave me a long funny look as if he thought, "Who do you think you're yelling at, Tin-Tooth?" and then he trotted off into the woods, not hurrying one bit.

It was almost dark, and to make it worse, it had begun to rain lightly. Something was rattling away in the woods like a jackhammer. I began to walk up and down, with the bow in one hand, the knife in the other, and an arrow between my teeth.

I nearly fell down with fright when something brushed past me, but it was only a squirrel. I kept looking up into the trees in case of mountain lions, and suddenly I saw these glowing eyes. I yelled and the arrow fell to the ground. I didn't dare stoop to pick it up. Then the eyes blinked shut and open and shut very fast and just as I was bracing myself for a mortal struggle, the creature said,

"Whoooo . . ." and rose up out of the tree. It was an owl. I felt like a fool.

"Marianne . . ." It was a voice right behind me.

I jumped.

"It's only me." A small shape rose out of the shadows: it was Dougie. Then a man appeared right behind him. I hadn't even heard them! If they had been hostiles, they could have scalped me before I ever knew they were there.

"I brung my uncle," Dougie said.

The uncle was a skinny little man with black hair that stood up straight. He grinned at me and nodded. "Howdy." He went over to the buck. He had some kind of canvas thing that he put the buck into, like a hammock. Then we started off through the dark woods. The buck's head hung out of the canvas just in front of me and once, when the uncle stopped for a second to get around a deadfall, I touched the smooth antlers. I thought: I'll always remember you, buck.

NINETEEN

THIS IS A CONTINUATION of the same day. I fell asleep in the middle of telling about it.

When I came into the house, Katherine was all set up to be mad. It was way past dinner time, and I imagine I looked like something the cat quite literally dragged in. But then she took a closer look and said, "What's the matter?"

"We have to rescue Oliver. He's in jail."

"Tell me about it. With as few embellishments as possible."

That hurt my feelings but then I remembered that she really cares about Oliver and she was probably upset. So I told her—with as few embellishments as possible.

Before I'd even finished, she was putting on her coat. "You'd better take a hot bath," she said, "so you won't catch cold. There's plenty of food in the refrigerator; warm something up."

"Where are you going?"

She looked surprised that I should ask. "To get Oliver out of jail." She opened the drawer of the table in the hall and stuffed some money in her pocket.

"Are you going to walk?" It's almost a mile to the jail.

"Of course," she said, very impatient.

"Why don't you call Dr. Francis?"

"He's on a baby case." She opened the door. It had begun to rain harder. I was glad the buck wasn't out there in the woods.

"I'm coming with you."

"No," she said, "you've had enough. You stay here."

"I'm coming." I didn't like to contradict her—Katherine is not a woman you contradict—but this *was* my show.

She looked at me, frowning. "Well, hurry then."

I was right behind her. In no time flat we got to the main street. Nobody was out, although there were lights in the bars and in the newspaper office. Katherine glanced into them as we went by, especially Hank's Bar and Grill, which is next door to the newspaper.

She was walking fast, limping a little more than usual, her cane tap-tapping on the wooden planks of the sidewalk. The rain slanted into our faces, and it was cold.

The town hall, where the jail is, was dark. "Try the door," Katherine said.

I ran up the brick steps and rattled the big iron door handle, but it was locked all right.

Before I even got down off the steps, Katherine had started around the side of the building where the jail part is.

Once, out of curiosity, I wandered in there to see what

122

it looked like. It's just two tiny connected cages that stand in the middle of a big empty room. Mostly they use them for drunks, hauled in for the night to sober up.

There was a dim light in the room where the cells are. It's kind of a half-basement, so the windows come right to the ground. Katherine bent over and whacked one of the windows with her cane. I thought she was going to break it.

"Maybe it's unlocked," I said. I leaned down and pulled on it. It flew up so unexpectedly that I lost my balance and sat down on the wet grass.

Katherine knelt down. She hadn't even stopped to put a hat on, and her hair was soaking wet. "Oliver, are you in there?"

"Yes, Mrs. Carter." He sounded perfectly calm. That's an exasperating thing about Oliver, his calmness.

"Well, I'm going to get you out."

"Okay. Thanks."

"Are you all right?"

"Sure."

I leaned down and stuck my head clear inside the window. You know what Oliver was doing? It's hard to believe. He was playing cards with the man in the next cage.

"He's playing cards," I said. It seemed like fiddling while Rome burned. Here we were, charging around in the rain to secure his constitutional rights and insure his freedom, and he was playing cards with the town drunk!

"Shut the window," Katherine said.

I tried, but I could only get it half way shut. I left it because she was already going down the street, tip-tap. I had to run to catch up.

She stopped at the Silver Dollar Bar (which doesn't have a single visible silver dollar in it) and said to the bartender, "Is Charlie Bell here?"

"No, Mrs. Carter," the man said. "Try Hank's."

"Thank you. Do you happen to know if Sheriff Alder is in town?"

"No, he ain't. He's to a rodeo down at Butte."

"Thank you."

The bar had swinging doors, the short ones, just like a TV western. You could hear them squeaking and swinging as we went on up the street. I felt like *Gunsmoke* for the first time since I'd come here. I was really enjoying it.

We found him in Hank's. He was sitting at the bar with a big glass of beer in his hand. He put it down when he saw Katherine.

"Well, Miz Carter," he said, in that insulting voice of his, "didn't know you hung out at Hank's."

"Release Oliver Everybodylooksat from that cell."

Her voice was the queen ordering one of her subjects to the Tower.

Some of the men sitting near Charlie, who'd begun to snicker, stopped snickering.

Charlie was obviously three sheets to the wind. He stood up, and although Katherine is a tall woman, he towered over her. I was afraid he was going to hit her, and I grabbed an empty beer bottle just in case. The bartender leaned over the counter and said, "Easy does it, Charlie."

Charlie made a mock bow and nearly fell over. "Madam," he said, "Madam the Great Lady, you can all rot in hell before I'll let that Injun out of jail. He beat up on my boy."

"Your 'boy' tried to steal his deer," I said. "So did you."

Katherine won't ever let me into the act. She silenced me with a look. "Give me the keys."

"Ha!" He looked around at the other men. But they were watching Katherine. She was giving a good performance; they were getting a free evening at the theater with their beer. " 'Gimme the keys,' she says. The Great Lady what won't hire me to work for her because she's a damned Injun lover . . ."

"Shut up, Charlie," the bartender said. "You're drunk."

"I'd run you in," Charlie said to Katherine, "only I ain't got an empty cell. I'd run you in for obstructin' the law."

"Give me the keys," Katherine said.

"Like hell." Charlie sat down and refilled his beer glass from the bottle. He had his back to Katherine.

The door opened, and Mr. Faber came in. He stood by the door watching. Katherine didn't even turn around. She said, "Mr. Morrissey, may I use your phone?"

"Sure, Ma'am." The bartender pulled a phone out from under the bar somewhere and put it on the counter.

"Thank you. Do you happen to know where the sheriff stays when he's in Butte?"

One of the men down the bar said, "The Finlen."

"Thank you." She dialed the operator and asked for a person-to-person call to the sheriff. "Put it on my bill," she said. "I'm Mrs. Carter."

There was absolute silence while she waited for the call to go through. Charlie was pretending to ignore the

whole thing, but he was beginning to look uneasy. He
fiddled with the empty bottle. I still had the one I picked
up. It's always just as well to stay armed until all the
danger is over.

"Sheriff?" Katherine's clear, vibrant voice filled the
barroom. "This is Katherine Carter." Briefly and without embellishments, she told him the story. "I want
Oliver released at once. Your assistant refuses to com-
ply." She was magnificent, even with her hair soaking
wet and kind of disheveled—in fact, that added drama.
She was authority.

After she had listened for a moment, she said, "Thank
you, Sheriff. . . . Yes, he's here." She handed the phone
to Charlie without a word.

I thought he wasn't going to pick it up. He looked at
it as if he thought it would bite. And I guess it did. When
he finally took it, he said, "Yeah, this is Charlie." Then
he listened for a minute. "Okay," he said, and hung up.

For a few seconds he just sat there, and everyone
waited. Then he whirled around on the bar stool and
faced Katherine, his head thrust forward like a tough
football player. "You just got me fired." Then he yelled
it. "You got me fired, you damned bitch!"

"All right, Charlie," the bartender said, "out you go."

"Shut up!" Charlie snarled at him.

"May I have the keys?" Katherine held out her hand.

He spat at it. Fortunately he missed. Some of the men
kind of half got up, and I heard Mr. Faber step forward,
but Katherine didn't need any help. She lifted her cane
and brought it down on the counter hard, about an inch
from Charlie's glass. The bang made some beer spill out
of the glass. "The keys!"

For a long moment they stared at each other. Then he

pulled a ring of keys off his belt and slammed them down on the counter and stormed out of the bar. There was a crash outside.

"Christ, he fell down the steps," one of the men said.

Mr. Faber looked out the door. "He's all right. He's heading for the Silver Dollar."

Katherine straightened her shoulders ever so slightly. "Thank you, Mr. Morrissey." She picked up the keys.

"Yes, ma'am." Mr. Morrissey's voice was very respectful.

Mr. Faber held the door open for us. "Can I help you get that place unlocked?" he asked. "Those old locks are kind of ornery."

The same voice at the back of the bar said, "Christ, she don't need no help."

"Thank you," Katherine said to Mr. Faber, and he walked with us in the rain to the town hall and unlocked the door. We went down the long hallway, with its nameplates for Town Clerk, Sheriff, Street Commissioner and all that. The place was cold, and it smelled like stale cigars. Mr. Faber found a light switch, and we went down a half flight of wooden steps to the room where the cells were. The drunk had fallen asleep, but Oliver was sitting there playing solitaire.

It seemed as if there ought to be a blast on the trumpets and a red velvet carpet thrown down, and the prisoner pressing his tearful face to the bars, crying, "You've saved me! Oh, your majesty, I shall be your slave forever." But Oliver put a red card on a black card, looked up, and said, "Hi."

"We've come to save you." I had to say it. *Somebody* had to.

Katherine looked at me. "What are you doing with

that beer bottle?" she said.

I was surprised to find it in my hand. "Oh," I said. It seemed silly now to explain. "I just happened to pick it up."

Mr. Faber was having trouble with the lock on the cell. He tried different keys.

Katherine laughed, and for the first time she sounded tense. Reaction, I guess. "What an anticlimax! Don't tell me we can't get him out."

"Maybe he gave you the wrong keys," I said.

Oliver reached through the bars. "Can I try, Mr. Faber?" He took the keys and after trying a couple, he got the lock open. He brushed off his jeans and put the cards down beside the drunk, who had never waked up.

"Thanks," he said to us. "It was getting pretty boring."

Mr. Faber gave us a ride home.

"You'd better stay here tonight," Katherine said to Oliver. "Charlie Bell is drunk and angry."

"Oh, I'll be all right."

"No, please, I would feel more secure."

"Well, all right. I'll sleep in the barn."

"Oliver, I have four empty bedrooms."

But he insisted on sleeping in the barn as usual. What a dumb attitude. Katherine lent him some blankets and a pillow and a toothbrush. He laughed when she gave him the toothbrush. His teeth are so white and even, he could probably go a month without brushing and still have pretty teeth. But he thanked her anyway. She made him come into the kitchen, and she fixed hamburgers and fried potatoes and coffee and sliced tomatoes. I was almost collapsing with hunger. But in the middle of the first bite of the hamburger, I remembered the deer.

"These aren't venison, are they?"

She gave me a nice smile. "No, just plain Swift and Company beef."

I had thought I'd never eat any meat again, but I couldn't control myself. I ate three hamburgers. Now Oliver is out in the barn, probably sleeping as if nothing had ever happened, and Katherine is reading in bed. I am dead tired. It's hard to imagine so much happening in one day. It will take a long time to sort it all out and see what it means. If anything.

TWENTY

IT WAS THREE-TWENTY by my little travel alarm
clock when I woke up with a jerk. It was dark in my
room, but outside the window there was a strange red
glow and the horses were screaming. Someone was
pounding on the door, and then I heard Oliver yell.
"The barn's on fire! Call the fire department!"

Katherine was already on the phone when I opened
my door. I pulled on some clothes, and she ran past me
and down the stairs.

I could hear the roar of the fire and that terrible con-
stant screaming of the horses, and I could smell the
smoke. I didn't know what to do.

When I got outside, I could see Oliver and Katherine
in the red light. The rain had stopped. Oliver was fight-
ing with the gelding, trying to get him out of the burning barn. The horse reared and slashed with his hoofs.
I'd heard that horses fight not to be taken out of a burn-

ing building, but I always thought it was an old wives' tale. It's true, though.

I screamed when I saw Katherine put her arm over her face and limp into the barn. I didn't think I'd ever see her again. Not alive, at least. I ran over to Oliver and tried to help him, but all I did was get in the way.

Oliver yelled, "Get back."

Then he hit the horse hard on the behind, and Cyrano bolted out of the barn at last and stopped under the big willow tree. I knew I should probably go and tie him up, but I couldn't leave the entrance of the barn. I was so worried. Oliver had dashed back in to help Katherine with the mare. A whole big piece of the roof fell blazing right at my feet and I got a shower of sparks in my face. I had to beat out a couple of places on my shirt that started to burn but I was hardly conscious of what I was doing, I was so scared about them. The smoke was choking me. I decided I had to go into the barn even though I'd probably louse everything up. But right then I saw Katherine and Oliver pulling on Candida. Katherine had her by the mane and Oliver was shoving her from behind. The poor little horse was screaming with fear.

Part of the loft fell in with a great roar and a burst of flame, and Candida reared. One of her front hoofs struck Katherine and knocked her down. The horse leaped over her and out of the barn. I ran into the barn, and Oliver and I got Katherine up and out of there. Almost as soon as we cleared the door, the rest of the roof fell in.

Katherine was hurt. She held onto her ribs and she looked white as death, but she wouldn't leave. Then I heard the blessed, blessed shriek of the fire engine siren.

Oliver yelled in my ear, "Go call Dr. Francis."

I ran in the house. First I couldn't find the phone book and second I was so nervous I couldn't dial it right.

I dialled the operator and when I tried to talk to her, I found I was sobbing. "Get Dr. Francis here quick," I said. My voice was so hoarse, she could hardly understand me.

"Where?" she said. "Where?"

"Mrs. Carter's. Fire. She's hurt." I hung up and fainted.

It's not very satisfactory to faint when there's nobody there to see you. Besides I had to see what was going on. So I pulled myself up off the floor and went outside.

The fire company was there, spraying long streams of water on the barn, but it was a lost cause. Most of the barn had already collapsed, and all the water did was to make a hideous muddy mess. I felt very bad; that barn was my refuge.

Katherine was sitting propped up against the tree with Oliver's jacket around her. She looked very pale, and there were streaks of smoke and soot on her hands and face and her bathrobe was burned in places. She was staring at the barn, and she didn't look up when I came over to her. Oliver was with her. He had some bad looking burns on his arms and across his neck and burned places in his shirt.

Dr. Francis arrived, squealing his tires he came into the yard so fast. He helped Katherine up and got her into the house. At the door he said, "Marianne, you and Oliver go into the kitchen. I want to look at you both after I've taken care of your grandmother. Give Oliver a shot of whiskey."

Oliver went back first to make sure the horses were all right. When he came in, I was fooling around with Katherine's Melitta coffee pot, which makes marvelous coffee and is really quite simple except that I am not very ept in the kitchen. My father says I am the only person he knows who can burn water. (That's a family joke.)

Oliver helped me with the coffee pot. "It takes great skill," he said. "What you do is this great engineering feat—you lift up a kettle of boiling water and pour it into the filter where the grounds are. See?" He was trying to joke because I guess he saw how shaky I was.

When he poured himself a shot of whiskey, he poured one for me, too, and added a lot of water. "You look like you need it."

I've sampled bourbon before, and I think it tastes like a low grade of paint remover, but it isn't quite as bad as scotch. I drank it down as fast as I could and gagged slightly and pretty soon I stopped shaking because it did warm my stomach up.

"I loved that barn," I said.

He shrugged. "A barn is a barn. The thing is, nobody got killed and the horses are all right.

"How did the fire start?"

He finished off his whiskey and squinted his eyes. "I can see it now. 'Drunken Indian falls asleep while smoking. Carter barn burns to the ground.' "

"But you weren't drunk and you don't smoke. Anyway, Mr. Faber wouldn't print a bunch of lies like that."

"No, you're right. Faber is okay."

"But how did it start?"

He didn't answer for a minute. Then he said, "Somebody set it."

I gasped. I hadn't thought of that. "Who?"

"I woke up when I heard glass breaking. It was that little window beyond the stalls. Then I smelled kerosene, and before I could get there a flaming pine branch came through the broken window. It hit the hay. In about two seconds the whole end of the barn was burning. I got the horses out of the stalls, but I couldn't get them out the door . . ."

"But who would have done such a thing?"

Again he didn't answer for a few minutes. "After the fire trucks came, I went out and looked at the ground— it's still wet from the rain. There were tire marks—very wide tires . . ."

"Like Patrick has on the dune-buggy?"

"I suppose a lot of people use those wide tires."

"But not a lot of people would want to burn Katherine's barn."

Dr. Francis came into the kitchen. "She broke a rib," he said. "She'll be all right. It hurts but I've got her taped up and in bed. We'll keep her there a while if we can. Now, let's look at you, Ollie."

After he'd fixed up Oliver, he looked me over. I didn't know it, but I had some burns, too. I don't know if they just hadn't begun to hurt or I was too wrought up to feel it. He daubed stuff on and gave me an aspirin.

"Now get to bed," he said. "I'm going to stay here all night, just in case. I suggest you stay, too, Oliver. Mrs. Carter says to remind you there are plenty of bedrooms."

"I'll sleep on the couch in the living room," Oliver said.

So all these people are asleep in the house; even Katherine's light is out now. The firemen have gone home and the smell of smoke is still heavy in the air. Evil has struck at us, and we have survived but none of us will ever be quite the same again.

TWENTY-ONE

KATHERINE'S RIB was still taped and it hurt her to take a deep breath but she insisted on going ahead with the reading at the church.

The parish room is big but it was packed full. I sat with Dr. Goodwin and Mr. Bartlett in the third row on the aisle. D and the other three were in the second row on the side and they kept looking at me and whispering to each other and snickering. I was a nervous wreck.

The first thing on the program was a guy with a guitar singing country music. I like country music, and he was pretty good except when he flatted. He got a lot of applause.

Then the minister read some poems by Robert W. Service, and that was okay except it went on too long and he got a little carried away. Have you ever noticed how a lot of ministers and other public speakers accent words like adverbs and prepositions, the words that don't really mean anything? This is the bane of my existence. Radio announcers do it all the time. Example: ". . . and *on* this occasion, the person *to* whom we give full credit. . . ." Like that.

When Mr. James finally delivered his last ringing line, Miss Alma Mitchell's Junior High Ballet did a few turns, swooping around the stage on their toes, in pastel colored cheesecloth. One girl swooped too hard, turned her ankle, and had to go limping offstage. You could see Miss Mitchell's hand sticking out, helping her off. That's the kind of thing that would happen to me, if I were even able to get up on my toes and swoop around in the first place, which is a ludicrous thought.

During the dancing, Patrick and two other big boys came in and sat in the back row, making a lot of noise. People shushed them, and they grinned like the apes they are. I was afraid they would cause a disturbance during Katherine's reading, but then I saw Sheriff Alder standing in the back, wearing his guns. He's even bigger than Patrick, although in my opinion, he's not much of a sheriff. It's true he fired Patrick's father, but when he came out to investigate the fire, he hardly paid any attention to what Oliver said. He didn't even seem to think it was for sure that the fire had been set. And, of course, the rain had washed away the tire tracks.

The last of Miss Mitchell's ballerinas tottered offstage, and it was time for Katherine. My hands were wet. I'd have given anything to leave right then. Mr. Bartlett tapped me on the arm and gave me a big smile. He seemed to be actually looking forward to it.

The stage went dark, and you could see the outlines of two people doing something to the scenery. They carried off the wallpaper-covered flat, all over birds and roses, that had been the backdrop for the ballet.

"Why don't they use the curtain?" I whispered to Mr. Bartlett.

"It got stuck last year when they did *Charley's Aunt,*" he said.

It got stuck last year! That's this town for you.

The guys who took off the flat brought in something and set it at the back of the stage; you couldn't see what it was but it was big and bulky. As they were running off, one of them tripped and fell flat. The audience gave him a big hand.

There was an interminable wait. I could hardly sit still, I was so nervous. I thought I might have to leave. But then those girls would really snicker.

Just at the point of complete unbearableness, a spotlight came on, and there was Dr. Francis standing on the apron of the stage. He was wearing a dark suit. I'd been afraid he'd turn up in a Roman toga and a wig and false whiskers that might fall off at the crucial moment, but he had on his own face.

"Ladies and Gentlemen," he said. "Mrs. Carter and I are going to do a short scene from Sophocles' play, *Antigone.* I would like to fill you in on what has happened. Antigone's uncle, Creon, is the ruler of Thebes. Antigone's two brothers have just been killed in a civil war in which they fought on opposite sides. One of them, who fought on Creon's side, has been buried with military honors. The other, Polyneices, who fought with the rebels, has been left where he fell, unburied, and Creon has said that anyone who tries to bury him will be killed. The religion of the Greeks made it a disgrace to leave a man unburied—he was dishonored by it. So Antigone steals out into the plains at night and makes a token burial of her brother, throwing dust on his body. Creon learns of it, and although she is his niece, he condemns Antigone to death. In the scene that we will do, the guards have brought the young princess Antigone before her uncle, Creon."

The light went off and Dr. Francis disappeared. "The *young* princess Antigone . . ." I could swear I heard tittering from the row where D and the others sat.

Then the lights came up on the stage. Toward the back there was a platform draped in black velvet, and a stool, also draped in black. Dr. Francis sat on the stool. He still had on his suit, of course, but now he had a short scarlet cape flung over his shoulders. Someone had done a good job with the lighting; it was soft and kind of luminous.

From offstage a man's voice spoke. It was the minister, and looking at the play now, I see he was supposed to be the sentry who brought the princess Antigone to Creon.

"We ran and took her at once. She was not afraid.
Not even when we charged her with what she had done. She denied nothing.
    And this was a comfort to me,
And some uneasiness; for it is a good thing to escape from death, but it is no great pleasure to bring death to a friend.
    Yet I always say there is nothing so comfortable as your own safe skin."

Then Katherine stumbled onstage, as if the sentry had pushed her. I caught my breath. She *did* look like a young princess! She was wearing a loose silvery silk robe with a blue sash that I had never seen. She'd let her hair go loose and it was like a dark cloud. This was my grandmother?

Creon (Dr. Francis) said:

> "And you, Antigone, you with your
> head hanging,—do you confess this thing?"

She lifted her head in a marvelous way and said:

> "I do. I deny nothing."

Creon looked at her for a few seconds before he spoke. It was nice timing—Katherine's idea, I suppose—you felt he really wished he hadn't gotten into this. If you've ever read *Oedipus the King,* you know Creon wasn't a bad man, just pig-headed.

> "Tell me, tell me briefly: Had you heard my
> proclamation touching this matter?"

Antigone looked him right in the eye.

> "It was public. Could I help hearing it?"

> "And yet you dared defy the law."

> "I dared. It was not God's proclamation. That final
> Justice that rules the world below makes no such
> laws."

She went on with the speech about the laws of God, and I tried to think of the word for her voice. Impassioned, I guess. It was vibrant with emotion, low and kind of pulsing. Even D and her friends were listening. This *was* a young princess who was going to be stoned to death for honoring her beloved brother.

"I know I must die, even without your decree:
I am only mortal. And if I must die
Now, before it is my time to die,
Surely this is no hardship: can anyone
Living, as I live, with evil all about me,
Think Death less than a friend? This death of mine
Is of no importance, but if I had left my brother
Lying in death unburied, I should have suffered.
Now I do not.
                    You smile at me. Ah, Creon,
Think me a fool, if you like; but it may well be
That a fool convicts me of folly."

Her whole body expressed her feelings, somehow; she was all pride, and integrity, and . . . oh, I don't know. I had to keep mopping the tears out of my eyes, hoping no one would notice.

And Creon was saying:

"The inflexible heart breaks first, the toughest iron
Cracks first, and the wildest horses bend their necks
At the pull of the smallest curb . . ."

But you knew, just from the very outline of Antigone's body, that he was wrong. His was the pride that would crack in the end. Their voices went on, saying the great lines.

Now Antigone was saying:

"Ah, Creon, Creon,
Which of us can say what the gods hold wicked?"

And Creon says:

"An enemy is an enemy, even dead."

Antigone made a beautiful outward gesture with her hand:

"It is my nature to join in love, not hate."

Creon rose up, looking very tall and terrible. It never occurred to me to think of him as Dr. Francis.

"Go join them, then; if you must have your love,
Find it in hell!"

The lights were cut and for about a whole minute there wasn't a sound in that dark room. Then the applause began and the foot-stamping and cheering, and when Katherine and Dr. Francis came out for a curtain call, everybody got to his feet, even D and the others. The applause went on for maybe five minutes. It wasn't until Mr. Bartlett offered me a large linen handkerchief that I realized tears were streaming down my face. Oh, Broadway, what you lost! Oh, Marianne, how blind you were!

Later there was a big party at our house with the minister and his wife and Miss Alma Mitchell and the guitar player and Mr. Faber, and of course the Saturday night regulars, plus a dozen people I didn't even know.

It was a marvelous party, and nobody told me to go to bed. I tried to make myself useful, passing *hors d'oeuvres* and potato chips and filling up the ice bucket. It was really gala, and Katherine was absolutely shining. Now I knew how she must have looked when she was on the stage. It must really do something for you, to be awfully good at something. I want terribly to be awfully good at something.

When they'd all gone, Katherine sank into a chair and then she looked tired. "Well, Marianne," she said, "was it all right?"

I had to measure my words rather carefully because I'd sneaked a brandy in the kitchen. "I think you are a magnificent actress, and I am proud to be your granddaughter. You were simply splen . . . you were splendid."

She laughed. "Thank you. That's nice to hear, especially since I know you are not given to idle flattery. You'd better go to bed now."

And when I got to the door, she said, "How did you like the brandy?"

I'll never know how she knew.

TWENTY-TWO

A VERY INTERESTING THING happened today at school. I was eating my chicken salad sandwich and sort of swinging a little on one of the little kids' swings, and here were A, B, C and D coming at me. Oh, no, I thought, not again. They've pretty much left me alone lately. They lined up in front of me, and for a few seconds nobody said anything. Then B poked D with her elbow. "Tell her," she said.

D looked funny, kind of pink. She said, "Uh, we saw your grandmother in that play at the church . . ."

"So?" I was as cold as possible. If they thought they were going to insult my grandmother, they had another think coming.

"Well," D said, looking down at her feet, "we thought she was terrific."

There was a moment of stunned silence while I mentally reeled.

144

"She really was," A said. "Man, she was beautiful. You'd never believe she was all that old."

"Well, she isn't all *that* old," I said, but I was beginning to feel awfully good. I had to play it cool of course—I mean, these had been my mortal enemies.

"But she *is* your grandmother," C said. "And she was more like a young girl. I mean glamorous and all."

"My mother says she thinks she remembers her in some old movies," B said.

I started to say she was never in any movies, but I decided not to. "I'm glad you enjoyed it," I said.

"Do you think she'd give lessons?" D said. "I mean, like to us?"

I was astounded. "Lessons? I don't know. I doubt it."

"Will you ask her?" D said. "Man, I'd really like to learn to act. I mean that was really out of sight."

"I'll be glad to ask her," I said.

The bell rang, and we had to go in. They walked to the room with me. Just before we went in, I said, "Would you guys like to come over to my house some afternoon after school? We could . . ." I tried to think what we could do. "We could play cards or something."

They accepted *en masse*. I worried all the rest of the afternoon about what Katherine would say. I told her at dinner, and for a second she frowned, but then she said, "Of course it's all right. I'll make some sandwiches and cocoa. What girls are they?"

When I told her their names, she said, "Isn't the Davis girl the one you hit?"

"Yes."

"Well, I'm glad you've reached a happier relationship."

"It's really you they want to see," I said. "They want you to give them acting lessons."

"Oh, my," she said. "I'm afraid I'm not ready for that." She took my plate and gave me some of this marvelous stuff that she makes with nothing but a couple of cans of minced clams and a few breadcrumbs and stuff. "Marianne, don't be afraid to believe that people like you. They're coming to see you, not me."

"They've been pretty mean to me up to now."

"Well, you were probably stand-offish. You *can* be rather frightening, you know."

"Really?" I didn't know whether to be pleased or not.

"Yes. You certainly scared me. I mean you're a rather formidable child."

(I looked it up a few minutes ago. "Formidable: causing dread, fear, or awe, hard to handle or overcome." The word just ahead of it in the dictionary is "formicate," meaning "to crawl or swarm with ants." I must work that into the conversation some time.)

She went on talking. "You have to take a chance, with friends or love or whatever—with art, too. You have to make yourself vulnerable."

I said, "Do you mean it's better to have loved and lost than never, etcetera?"

She smiled. "Exactly."

Well, she may be right. I'll have to think about it. Anyway the girls will be coming over on Friday, I guess.

TWENTY-THREE

ON THURSDAY I stopped by the newspaper office after school to tell Mr. Faber how nice I thought his review of Katherine's performance was. Of course, it wasn't a review like *The New York Times* or the Boston *Herald*—it was more of a news story about the whole show—but he said very nice things about how lucky the town was to have Mrs. Ben Carter in their midst and how she gave a "luminous performance of a moving role" and how people who carry on about the protests of the young ought to read the rest of *Antigone,* especially the dialogue between Creon and his son, who was in love with Antigone and killed himself when she died. I say "amen" to that. One little bit I really like is when Creon says:

> "You consider it right for a man of my years and
>   experience
> To go to school to a boy?"

And his son says:

"It is not right
If I am wrong. But if I am young, and right,
What does my age matter?"

In my humble opinion that's really socking it to 'em.

I asked Mr. Faber why he didn't ever print my letter protesting injustice to the Indian. He gave me a look, with eyes half-squinted shut. "Well, Marianne," he said, "I presumed you were referring to Oliver, am I right?"

"Oliver was the immediate example."

"Yes. Well, I didn't print it because I like Oliver, and most of the other Indians in our town."

"What sense does that make?" I said.

"I was afraid it might exacerbate their troubles."

I like that word "exacerbate." I'd never heard anyone use it before. "How?"

"By stirring up an anti-Indian backlash. Your letter is so general, if you'll forgive me for saying so, that it would not solve any particular problem, and all it might do is to make the wrong people mad."

"But Oliver didn't get a fair deal.'

"I know. Name me an Indian that does. But goading people won't help. Oliver is in a particular pickle because he's a bright boy and he's going to become an educated man, an expert, and people who are stupid hate an expert, especially if he happens to be a member of a race they consider inferior to their own. Ask any black man; he knows the problem well. Or a Mexican-American. If Oliver got into a specific kind of trouble that he couldn't get himself out of, believe me, I'd go to bat for him all the way. But I think he's handling things very well. He is quiet and he doesn't make waves when it isn't necessary, but he'll get where he wants to go."

I was impressed. "I guess I was wrong," I said. I don't say that too often, at least not out loud. In fact, it's only lately I've begun to notice it.

"Your heart's in the right place, Marianne," he said. "You're going to be a good woman to have in this cock-eyed world. When we're young, we have to learn when to fish, and when to cut bait, but you're going to be all right—just fine." He gave me an extra copy of the paper with the review of Katherine. "You might want it for your scrapbook. Remember me to your grandmother. She's a fine woman, a real artist."

Mr. Faber is a discerning man. He ought to get the Pulitzer Prize. I wonder how you go about suggesting people for the Pulitzer Prize? Maybe if I wrote the committee a letter . . .

But I haven't had much time to think about it because today was the day the girls came to visit me. Alice, Polly, Kim and Doris. We played Darts in the basement a while, and then we came upstairs and played Gin Rummy and Katherine brought us some terrific tea sandwiches and frothy cocoa with no scum on it. The girls were terribly awed, and they didn't dare ask her if she'd give them lessons, but I told them I didn't think she would.

"I'll bet she gives them to you," Polly said.

I smiled a kind of remote smile and didn't say anything. Sometimes the most effective thing is not to say anything. I've just begun to discover that.

We had a good time and when they were going home,

Doris tried to flirt with Oliver, who was feeding the horses, and I didn't even mind. I was more amused.

After they'd gone, Oliver said, "Well, I see the Christmas season has started early. Peace and goodwill and all that."

"Don't be cynical," I said, and he laughed. He pitched some hay into the shed that he built after the barn burned. "Katherine said you're going over to the university Monday," I said.

"Yep. Got to see about that scholarship."

"I hope you get it."

He laughed again. "Thanks. Have you decided I'm a deserving redskin?"

"You're a nut," I said. But I've really gotten quite fond of Oliver. People all around town suddenly seem a lot nicer. Maybe I'm just living in reflected glory, from Katherine, but I'll try to think positively and assume that all this friendliness is because of my own devastating charms.

TWENTY-FOUR

TODAY IS SATURDAY, and looking back to this morning I feel as if it's years away. How is it some days propel you several light-years into the future, and other days are just a drag?

The mail comes in the morning, and this time I went out to the box to get it. There was a letter from my mother addressed to me and another one for Katherine. Katherine had gone to Kalispell to do some shopping, with Oliver driving her in the Chevrolet. She asked me if I wanted to go, but I hate shopping and I didn't want to get up that early.

I brought the letter into the house and propped it up on the kitchen table while I got myself some juice and several slices of Katherine's marvelous date bread and a glass of milk. For some reason I went upstairs and put on my gunbelt before I started to eat. I haven't worn the gunbelt for quite a while.

I drank my juice and ate two pieces of bread and drank a glass of milk before I opened the letter. To tell you the truth, I didn't want to open it. I hadn't heard from my mother since I got that note from Dad, and I guess I was afraid of what she'd say. It's surprising how hard you can be thinking about something that you don't think you're thinking about at all.

Well, I opened it finally and it said: "Dearest Marianne: This is a difficult letter to write." I should have stopped reading it right there. Never read a letter that starts out that way. But I kept on. "As you must know, your father and I have had our problems over the last few years. Our trip to Europe was a last attempt to get things straightened out, but it grieves me to say it didn't turn out well. Your father and I have finally, with the greatest reluctance in the world, agreed to a divorce." I put the letter down and took one of the guns out of my gunbelt and powed at the vase of flowers on the windowsill. Pow! Pow!

What was she telling me all this junk for? What did it have to do with me? Pow! My friends are Oliver Everybodylooksat and Dougie Three-Toes and Mrs. Foxtail and Mr. Faber and Mr. Bartlett. And Alice, Polly, Kim and Doris. I have my own life to live—you worry about yours. Pow! Pow! I have Dr. Francis. Pow! Even Dr. Goodwin. And Katherine—yes, especially Katherine.

But you can't let a letter just sit there unread. So I finished it. "Uncle George has been here with me, and as I am sure you are aware, he has wanted me to marry him for a long time." How should I be aware? Doorbells ringing, people pressing their foreheads against cold window panes, what the hell does all that have to do with me? "We three . . . safe as can be . . ." that's kid stuff. This is the real world. Get tough; act your age; look out for yourself.

I discovered I was crying, and that made me mad. I mopped my face and finished the damned stupid letter. "But I am not at all sure I want to risk it a second time." Risk, risk. It's a risk to get up in the morning. "So I have sent him away, for now, at least. I hope you'll understand me, Marianne, and forgive me. I was so lonely when your father was gone so much. Maybe it was symptomatic." Maybe *what* was symptomatic? Symptomatic of what? If there's anything I can't stand, it's 'it' used without a reference. "As soon as the legalities are taken care of, I'll come for you and we'll make a life together."

Don't bother. *Don't bother.* Make your own stupid life.

I got Katherine's leather punch and made a new hole in my gunbelt so it wouldn't fall down all the time. It never has fit just right.

I was half way out to Oliver's house before I remembered he wasn't there, but I went on anyway. Dougie was sitting on the front step crying. Mrs. Foxtail wasn't there —gone into town or something.

"What's the matter?" I said.

Dougie looked at me with mournful eyes. "My rooster is dead."

That was the last straw. It wasn't fair that Dougie's rooster was dead. A kid like Dougie doesn't ask for much. What kind of a God is it that kills off pet roosters of little boys? "What happened to him?"

He wiped his face on his sleeve. His nose was runny so

I gave him a Kleenex. "The buffalo ghost took him."

"Dougie, there isn't any buffalo ghost."

His eyes were very round. "Oh yes, Marianne, there is. Don't say that."

I didn't argue with him; it was no time for that. I put my arm around him and said, "I'm sorry, Dougie."

He leaned his head against my shoulder.

I tried to think how to comfort him.

"Want to go out and feed the osprey?"

"Without Oliver?"

"Sure. We can make it." What was I saying? But he did look cheered up.

He went to the well, hauled up a couple of fish and put them in his backpack and off we went.

It was a coolish day but sunny. I could see a thin plume of smoke from the ranger cabin, off in the woods. The long fall would be over pretty soon, and I wondered if I'd get to stay here long enough to see the real winter. I'd really like to. Oliver has talked about how the heavy snow looks on the trees, and it must be something. He says sometimes when there isn't even any snow at all, everything is covered with frost, like silver. I'd like to see that. But who knows where I'll be? There ought to be a Bill of Rights for children. They get moved around like pieces of chess.

"What are you crying for?" Dougie said. "Are you crying for my rooster?"

"Sort of," I said. He took hold of my hand. He has a cute hand, very square and brown, with dimples where you'd expect knuckles. Maybe all little kids have hands like that; I wouldn't know. I let him wear my gunbelt. It even fit him.

When we got to the lake, I helped Dougie turn the boat over so we could get in. I was getting more and more dubious about the whole expedition. Dougie was awfully little to be rowing a boat. But it had been my idea, so I had to go through with it.

Well, it turned out that he didn't really row. He sat in the stern with one oar and he kind of paddled. The boat did a lot of yawing, if that's the right word, and I was afraid we'd never make it, but we did. The water was still and gray.

When I got out of the boat, a thought struck me, "Dougie, can you swim?"

"Nope."

Great! I thought maybe we just ought to settle down on the island for life. I didn't know how I could face the trip back, with a little kid who couldn't swim. What if he fell overboard? He'd drown.

"We shouldn't have come out here without Oliver," I said.

"He can't swim either."

That's hard to believe, but I suppose it's possible. I have known grown men who couldn't swim—my father, for one. "We should all wear flotation jackets," I said. "I think it's the law."

"What's them?" he asked, and when I tried to explain, he just shook his head as if the ways of the white man were too much for him. Sometimes they're too much for me, for that matter.

At first we couldn't find the osprey. He wasn't hanging around the dead tree, the way he usually does. Then Dougie got very excited and teetered up and down on his toes. "Hey, look!" he cried. The osprey came in, flying low over the water.

"He's better!" I said.

He was still kind of awkward, though, and we were glad we'd brought him some fish. He lit on a rocky ledge around the other side of the island. It was kind of hard to get at, but no matter how much Dougie called him, he wouldn't come off that ledge. He would have come for Oliver.

A bunch of ducks flew by the boat and out of sight. I think they were what are called red-headed ducks. (I am interested in ducks, and I bought a little book about them at the store.) They have red heads, naturally, black chests, and they're white underneath and gray on their backs. I watched them out of sight. I don't know why I love ducks so much.

When I looked back, Dougie was climbing the ledge up to where the osprey was. I was kind of scared because it's a jaggedy kind of ledge and it juts out over the water. I was afraid he'd slip and fall in, but he was shinnying up there like a little mountain goat. The osprey watched him and lifted up his wings as if to say, "Hey, glad you dropped in for lunch." I hoped he wouldn't fly away before Dougie got there. Oliver would be glad to hear he could get around some.

Dougie made it to the top and took off his backpack and got out the fish, with the osprey nosing around him like an old hen after corn. Dougie gave him the fish and then he hunkered down on his heels to watch him eat it.

All of a sudden there was a shot. It sounded loud and near, and at the same instant the ducks rose up with a great rustle of wings and took off. Dougie threw himself flat, and all I could see was his hat.

A rubber boat came around the island. It was Patrick, and he had a dead duck.

The osprey lifted up off the ground, and Patrick saw it. He fired at it. At the time I thought he'd hit it because the osprey kind of flapped back onto the ground again, but it may have been just grazed. Patrick fired again, and just before the second bang, Dougie threw himself toward the osprey to protect him. It all happened so fast. I'm not absolutely sure how it was, but there was the smashing sound of the shotgun, and the osprey rose up into the air with a great beating of wings, and Dougie grabbed himself in the shoulder and fell backward off the ledge into the lake.

He made a splash of silvery water when he landed. I tried to yell, but I couldn't make a sound. Patrick was shading his eyes and looking into the sun after the osprey. I'm not sure he ever saw Dougie. He took off down the lake.

Dougie surfaced and then bobbed out of sight again. I hauled off my boots and ran into the water. It was shallow for a little bit and then it shelved off really deep. I could see Dougie, just below the surface. I had to do it, no matter how scary it was. I took a deep breath and stepped off the shelf. I got to him in just a couple of seconds, and I got hold of his hair first and then his jacket. I kept going under myself, and I was choking. It was just the way it was that time at camp, thinking for sure I was drowning.

I tried to keep my head and remember about Elementary Life Saving, but I couldn't think of any of it. I started treading water to keep myself up, and I got

Dougie under the arms, and very very slowly I pulled him toward shore. At first I thought "what luck that he isn't struggling," but then I realized what that might mean, and I was so scared I almost let go.

I fought to keep his head above water, but sometimes I couldn't keep my own head above water. My clothes weighed a ton. I felt as if my lungs would burst, and I really did think my end had come. I remember thinking I'd never know whether Oliver got his scholarship or not.

Then—I could hardly believe it—I felt the gravel under my feet and I was able to stand up. I carried Dougie to a clean sandy place and put him down. He was very heavy, and I remember thinking "dead weight" and being terrified by the words.

His eyes were kind of rolled back, and his lips were blue. He didn't seem to be breathing. At first I tried to remember how you did artificial respiration, but then I remembered he'd been shot and it might not be the right thing to do. I couldn't see a wound or any blood at first, but then I did. The water had washed away the first of it, but there was a stain below his right shoulder. I was afraid he might have been hit in the lung or something; even so I had to do something to get him breathing, or try to anyway. I put my mouth against his and breathed into it, trying to keep my breathing regular although actually I was gasping. His face felt very cold, and I thought it was probably all in vain, but I kept it up anyway.

Then he moved his head a little and choked, and a little stream of water ran out of his mouth. His eyes fluttered open and closed again. I turned his head more to the side so he wouldn't choke.

I was so happy he was alive. I stood up and looked at the sky, and I saw the osprey, far up, gliding in big circles. It was a sign. Oliver had saved the osprey, and I was going to save Dougie.

I kept saying out loud, "Marianne, keep your head." I thought about what to do. Don't move him. Cover him up, take the boat, and go for help. Where? The nearest place was the ranger cabin, although he might very well not be there. But a ranger cabin would have some kind of telephone or something, wouldn't it?

I squeezed the water out of my sweater and put it over Dougie, although I don't suppose a sodden wool sweater was much use. I guess dry leaves would have been better, but I didn't think of it. He was still wearing my gunbelt, and that was almost more than I could bear. I knelt beside him and said, "Dougie, I'm going for help. Just lie quiet, Dougie, and I'll bring somebody to take care of you. Trust me." But he didn't open his eyes or show any signs of having heard me.

Now the boat. The only time I'd ever rowed a boat was at camp, and they made me quit because I kept losing the oars. This time I couldn't afford to lose the oars.

Pushing the boat into the water, the way Oliver did, I waded out a little bit and then climbed in. I am not a graceful Indian, however; I almost tipped the boat over. But I made it to the middle seat, and I got the oars in the oarlocks. A little breeze had come up and small waves slapped the sides of the boat. It was blowing downlake, and I had to keep pulling harder on the downlake oar to keep more or less on course. I was shivering so hard, I nearly fell off the seat. I used the dead tree on the island as a guidepost, because I once asked Oliver how he could row straight for shore without looking where he was going, and he said that's how he did it.

But the oars were heavy, and I kept dipping them either too deep or too shallow, and a couple of times when I dipped too shallow I nearly lost the oars. Water was leaking in the bottom of the boat, too. Dougie usually bails, but I couldn't bail and row both.

Once I pulled too hard and an oar did come out of the oarlock. I didn't lose it, but I nearly fell over backward, and the boat veered way around in the wrong direction.

It's not really very far from the island to shore but it seemed like a thousand miles. I tried to think of the words of *How They Brought the Good News from Ghent to Aix,* but I couldn't remember them, and I didn't have time to concentrate on anything but those darned oars. Dip, pull, lift. My clothes were soaking wet, of course; and I was so cold and wet, I almost dropped the handles of the oars.

After about four hundred years, I felt the bow of the boat scrape bottom. For a moment I thought I'd landed on a reef or something, but I looked around and I was *there.* It wasn't exactly where Oliver beaches the boat, but it was close. I jumped out and pulled the boat up and ran for the ranger's cabin.

I am not a good runner. I crash into things, and I fall down. But I kept getting up and running some more. I prayed I would remember just where the cabin was; it wasn't too easy to tell, in the woods, but I stayed on that little game trail that Oliver follows and I thought I remembered the bunch of birch trees where you turn off to the cabin. I prayed to God, I prayed to Buddha, and I prayed to the Buffalo Ghost.

Finally I came to a clump of birch trees, in fact, I came to them in a very emphatic way; I tripped over a root and fell head-first into the birch trees. Before I had time to get into a fit of indecision about whether they were the right birch trees, somebody picked me up off the ground and said, "Where are you going in such a hurry?"

It was the ranger, and I could have kissed him. I grabbed his hand and tried to pull him along with me and babbled the story all at once. He said later that I was crying my eyes out but I didn't know it then. He made me stand still and he gave me a huge handkerchief to wipe my face and he said, "Now take a deep breath and tell me slow and easy."

My teeth were chattering so bad I could hardly talk, but I told him the best I could.

"All right. Come with me."

I wanted him to go to the island that very second, but he took me to his cabin, which wasn't far, and he used his little radio to call somebody and tell them he was bringing in a little boy that had been shot. Then he tossed a blanket at me and pointed to a pot of coffee that was steaming away on a little camp stove, and he was gone.

Dougie is in the hospital now, and Dr. Francis says he's going to be all right. He had a lot of internal bleeding but the shot didn't hit any vital parts. Dr. Francis says he's got my gunbelt under his pillow, which must be kind of uncomfortable.

I'm in bed and Katherine brought me my dinner and a hot toddy with a teaspoonful of rum in it so I could stop shivering. I'm getting sleepier and . . .

TWENTY-FIVE

THIS WAS MY DAY OF GLORY. Mr. Faber wrote up the story about how I saved Dougie and he suggested me for the town's annual Youth Gets Involved award. Last year it went to a boy who hauled somebody out of a burning car. They don't realize that I only did it because I didn't have any choice and I was scared to death and not brave at all. But it's pleasant to be a heroine even if only for a day.

At school the teacher congratulated me publicly, and after class my four friends carried on like I was Joan of Arc.

Nobody knows where Patrick is. After the story came out in the paper, he and his father moved out, bag and baggage. I made it perfectly clear in the story that I didn't think Patrick even knew what had happened. But I guess he was scared he'd be blamed. Poor Patrick; he's a repulsive oaf but I feel kind of sorry. Maybe I should have said I didn't know who it was with the gun.

Dougie is feeling better, and he's pleased with his bandage. I'm letting him keep the gunbelt, and Oliver went out to the island and found his hat.

TWENTY-SIX

WHEN I CAME IN just before dinner today, Katherine called me into the kitchen. She was making lasagne, and it smelled great. I was very hungry.

"Your mother called."

"Oh," I said. She hadn't mentioned hearing from her when I got my letter, and I had just tried to put my letter right out of my mind.

She leaned against the table, her hands all floury. "She says she told you about the divorce."

"Yes, I guess she did."

She looked at me a minute. "It's a pity."

I shrugged. "It's her life."

"She's leaving for home. She is anxious to see you."

All I felt was tired. "Big deal."

"I know how you must feel."

"I don't feel at all. I'm all felt out."

"She'll be here to get you on Saturday."

I felt as if I'd just touched a live wire. *"This* Saturday?"

She nodded. She turned her head away and patted the pasta and sprinkled flour on it. For a minute or so I just held my breath the way I used to do when I was a kid until I turned blue. Then I went into the wildest temper tantrum I've thrown in seven or eight years. Even while I was doing it, I kept thinking that Katherine would be revolted. But after a couple of minutes she put her arm around me and just held me like that without saying a word.

Pretty soon I tapered off. "I won't go," I said.

She got a white linen handkerchief from her pocket and wiped my face. I'll never forget that handkerchief; it had pink embroidered rosebuds. You don't see handkerchiefs much any more. "She's your mother," she said. "She needs you."

"She dumped me when I was in the way."

"That isn't fair. She's had a rough time."

"She never gave me a thought. Well, all right. This is my home now."

She caught her breath and then she looked away quickly. "I'm happy that you feel that way but she's your mother."

"I know she's my mother; you don't have to keep telling me that. What's so great about being a mother? I mean that doesn't mean your children are your slaves. I have my own feelings."

"I'll ask her if you can spend the summer with me, if you still want to when the time comes." She dropped her arm from my shoulders and took on a brisk tone. "Now then, will you wash up and set the table for me?"

"She'll marry Uncle George, and then she'll dump me again."

"Marianne, she didn't dump you. Stop using that silly word. Now go wash your face."

I did, and I set the table, and she was still messing around in the kitchen so I went outside. Oliver was finishing up the chores.

"Was that you, yelling up a storm?"

"It was."

He looked at me sharply. "What's wrong?"

"I have to go back East with my mother. Saturday." I was afraid I was going to cry again, but I didn't.

He didn't say anything, but after a few minutes he came over and sat beside me on the steps. "I'm sorry to hear that."

"Oh, I imagine you'll survive," I said.

"Yes, I imagine I will. But I like having you around."

I couldn't believe it. "You're just being sarcastic."

He chuckled. "No. You're a pest sometimes, and you're stubborn as ten mules, but you keep things popping around here." He picked up a dead leaf and poked out the stuff around the veins and let it crumble. "Your grandmother will be very lonesome."

I hadn't even thought of that. "Oh, I don't think so. I'm more of a bother than anything."

"Maybe at first, because she wasn't used to having a kid around, but she likes you a lot. She'll miss you."

Katherine opened the kitchen window and told me dinner was ready. "Join us, Oliver?"

"I guess I can't tonight, thanks just the same."

They go through that little routine every now and then, like a ritual or something.

I got up. "Thanks for being nice." I felt stupid saying it, but I wanted to anyway.

He grinned, with those gorgeous white teeth. "I can't help myself. I'm just such a doggone nice redskin."

At dinner I apologized to Katherine for my temper tantrum.

She nodded. "It's probably the last one you'll ever have." Then she got that kind of mischievous gleam in her eye that she gets once in a while. "It certainly was an impressive performance."

"I know," I said. "I'm afraid I'm rather good at it."

She leaned over and patted my hand. "I think you and I have more in common than either of us ever suspected."

That was a funny thing to say, all right. This beautiful woman with all this talent and glamor having anything in common with me. I said so, and she didn't say a thing, but she leaned across the table and kissed me.

So this is probably the last tape I'll make from Montana. I'll be packing and all that. Dr. Francis and the other two men are giving a little party for me tomorrow night, and in the afternoon I'm going out to the island one last time with Oliver, to take some pictures for auld lang syne. I've given him a stamped addressed post card so he can let me know about the scholarship.

And then it will be Saturday—the arrival of my mother, big fuss, lots of breathless chatter and the smell of Estee Lauder, and off to Boston on Sunday, back to the smog and traffic and noise and pigeons in the park. Back to a dying nation.

It has occurred to me just this very minute that maybe

the reason my mother is so flighty and kind of unreliable might be because *her* mother was so beautiful and talented. I mean that must have been hard to live up to. Because my mother is pretty but she really doesn't have anything terrific to offer, in my opinion. Maybe if I work at it, I can give her a little self-confidence so she won't have to throw herself away on Uncle George.

I look around this room. I will never forget one thing in it, not one. Even the scratch on the headboard of the bed I'll remember, and the slightly faded place on the wallpaper where Katherine must have moved a picture. And as soon as I can make it, I'll be back. Someday I'll come here and live in this house; I feel it in my bones. Oliver will be grown and gone, and the gunbelt won't fit Dougie any more; Katherine will be old or even dead and the osprey will be gone. But with any luck the island will be there, and the forest and the lake, and other ospreys, other deer, other owls that look like mountain lions in the dark. And I'll be someone else too, and yet the same.